THE BACKWARD BRIDE

BOOKS BY AUBREY MENEN

———

THE BACKWARD BRIDE
THE STUMBLING STONE
THE PREVALENCE OF WITCHES

———

CHARLES SCRIBNER'S SONS

The Backward Bride

A SICILIAN SCHERZO

BY

AUBREY MENEN

NEW YORK
CHARLES SCRIBNER'S SONS
1950

FOR
PHILIP DALLAS

CONTENTS

THE BACKWARD BRIDE

CHAPTER I

SICILIAN WEDDING

WITHOUT doubt Giorgio Morales was at the top of his profession. Everybody admitted that he was the most famous brigand in Sicily; and he was certainly the most popular. Even to the police he was known as "Uncle Giorgio," but from a respectful distance. For five years no policeman had dared to set foot in Monte Tauro, the tiny but beautiful town perched on mountains by the sea that Uncle Giorgio had made his headquarters.

Uncle Giorgio was everything that a good brigand should be. He was widely experienced—he had served his apprenticeship in New York—he was a dead shot at seven hundred yards; he observed the classic rule of robbing the rich and giving to the poor and, above all, he did not look in the least like a brigand. He was short, inclined to plumpness, and he wore a straggling grey moustache. His appearance was so undistinguished that nobody, once having seen him, could possibly remember him.

It is true that his pictures had appeared in the newspapers, especially one in which he sat dashingly upon a white horse. But that was not Uncle Giorgio. It was a young man called Orlando who looked every inch a brigand and in fact, when he was not posing for photographs, kept Uncle Giorgio's accounts. Orlando had a head for figures and some talent for book-keeping of a simple sort. He was a good fellow but a very bad shot. Uncle Giorgio liked him, but not as much as he liked Aquila.

Aquila was his favorite nephew. Aquila was twenty. He was not a brigand. He was an undergraduate at Palermo University (Uncle Giorgio paid the fees) and was generally considered to be the most promising student of his year.

It was therefore all the more surprising when Aquila married Anisetta. She was undoubtedly beautiful, but equally without doubt, she was very ignorant. She had been educated by Sicilian nuns who had themselves been educated by a saintly woman who believed in the maxim that a young girl should be good and let who will be clever.

Anisetta had an oval face, great black eyes, glossy hair, and a beautiful figure. She had the bare ability to read and write, but from preference she did neither. She was, as everybody in Monte Tauro said, a simple Sicilian.

But Aquila had loved her since she was ten and so they were married.

*   *   *

They were married in the Church of San Giuseppe by a priest whom Uncle Giorgio had seen through the seminary with a generous allowance. The priest took his duties very seriously, giving none of the brigands absolution until he was quite sure that they were really sorry for what they had done. Had he only known it, his zeal was wasted because he had been excommunicated by the Bishop of Messina. However, since he did not go to Messina and the brigands would never allow the Bishop or anyone else within ten miles of Monte Tauro, his excommunication bothered nobody, least of all Anisetta.

She was very serious in church and radiant when she came outside. Aquila was serious all the time, because he was a serious boy. Besides, he was progressively-minded and habitually worried a great deal about the sad state of the world. Anisetta worried only about the train of her wedding-dress, but she need not have done, because it behaved beautifully.

Uncle Giorgio was best man (as, indeed, when was he not?) and although a stranger would never have picked him out from the crowd, his brigands did, and gave him a tremendous cheer as he came out of the church.

His brigands looked very fine. Their boots gleamed in the

sunlight and their brass buttons were dazzling. By a happy thought they were all dressed as policemen, and as everybody who has seen an opera knows, an Italian policeman's full-dress uniform, when clean, is a very showy affair.

The uniforms had been bought by Uncle Giorgio on the occasion of an assault by five thousand policemen on Uncle Giorgio's mountain stronghold * which—although I shall give away no secrets—was not so very far from Monte Tauro itself. These five thousand policemen had been sent from Rome because the new democratic government considered that Uncle Giorgio was a public enemy.

Uncle Giorgio never lost his temper but on this occasion he had been very annoyed. He wrote to all the newspapers in Sicily asking them to compare, like fair men, the politics of Uncle Giorgio and the politics of the democratic government. Uncle Giorgio had said that he made no boasts; he did not maintain that his politics were better, he merely claimed that they were the same. Since both he and the government maintained themselves in power by robbing the rich and giving to the poor, less a deduction for administrative expenses, Uncle Giorgio claimed that the proposed police attack on him was motivated merely by professional jealousy.

The letter was widely published (with a photograph of Orlando on a white horse, as usual) and well received by the Sicilians. The police made their attack, but they felt that the ground had been cut from underneath their feet. Besides, the campaign grew very confused. The Chief of Police in Rome had with some subtlety dressed a large proportion of his forces as brigands. Uncle Giorgio, with the simplicity that marks all great men, had retaliated by dressing a large part of *his* forces as policemen.

Thus very early on, many police squads found themselves toiling up mountain-sides only to find at the top a squad of policemen already in possession. They dutifully made their report, and descended, many of them happy in the thought

* A device, like others narrated in this book, also adopted by the well-known bandit Signore Giuliano of Monte Lepre, near Palermo.

that they were going to be recommended for promotion—for the brigands bore the police no malice.

In a short space of time the police were withdrawn and the whole thing would have been forgotten by the Monte Taurans, if it had not been for the uniforms.

These had been regretfully put away in trunks (for Uncle Giorgio did not believe in deceit unless he was driven to it). But everybody was very glad of the opportunity to wear them, so now the brigands made a gallant and happy showing as they escorted their beloved chief, his nephew, and his nephew's beautiful bride along the narrow streets to the Café Orologio where the wedding breakfast was all set out and waiting.

* * *

The wedding presents were laid out on a side table. There were the usual presents from the brigands: pearls, sapphire drop-earrings, and more gold watches than Aquila would know what to do with. These excited little comment. But the present from Aquila's University class-mates was much admired.

It was a handsomely bound set of the complete works of the man whom Aquila admired above all living thinkers, the celebrated British philosopher and renowned broadcaster, Professor Francis Lissom.

Since this book is written in English, there is no need to enlarge upon Lissom's fame. Merely to recite the titles on the backs of the books will remind every progressive reader of the man who has liberated sex, family life and marriage from the shackles of Victorian morality; nay, any morality whatever. Who has not read *Morals for Moderns?* or *Do Children Need Parents?* or *This Age of Freedom?* If there be any such, then they will nevertheless have come into contact with Lissom's intensely contemporary and fearless mind in his world-famous question-and-answer broadcasts "Tell me, Professor" and his more formal but none the less stimulating broadcasts "Twentieth Century Lectures."

Aquila knew whole pages by heart. On all hands it was

considered a most apt present. But even this was not the center of comment.

What everybody was pointing out to everybody else was that there was nothing from Uncle Giorgio.

Curious—though respectful—glances were cast at him. But Giorgio, as was his custom, said nothing. He smoked his pipe, and smiled.

Champagne was served.

Still Uncle Giorgio said nothing.

Cassata alla Siciliana was served.

Uncle Giorgio ate some with relish, but still said nothing.

And then, just when the mandolin orchestra was tuning up for the first dance to begin as a sign that the formal breakfast was over, Uncle Giorgio knocked out his pipe and said:

"Oh, I almost forgot."

He spoke quietly, but instantly brigands standing near hushed down the other guests.

He put his hand in his pocket.

"Aquila," he said, "here is something for you and your charming bride."

He handed Aquila an envelope.

Aquila looked at it hesitantly.

"It's a *cheque*," said one of the less self-controlled of the guests.

But Aquila knew that it could not be. Although Uncle Giorgio often had dealings with various branches of the Bank of Sicily, they were more in the nature of withdrawals than deposits.

"Open it, my boy," said Uncle Giorgio.

Aquila did so. He drew out a very slim book, gold stamped on the cover.

He opened it.

"A passport!" he said, overwhelmed. "For my wife and me!" He turned the pages. "A visa for England!" he exclaimed. "Does that mean . . ." he said, looking at his uncle, and scarcely daring to name his hope.

"Yes," said Uncle Giorgio, his eyes twinkling with pleasure. "I am going to take you and Anisetta on a little holiday. It occurred to me that you might like to meet this Professor Francis Lissom in person."

*　　*　　*

Once again Uncle Giorgio had done the exactly right thing in the most admirable manner. The general satisfaction was audible.

"*Thank* you," said Aquila fervently.

"Don't thank me," said Uncle Giorgio, filling his pipe again. "Thank your Uncle Domenico. He engraved it."

Uncle Domenico was much more distinguished looking than his famous brigand brother, but he was even more modest.

While the guests and Aquila congratulated Domenico, he blushingly fussed with a great bowl of ice-cream, measuring out portions and putting them on small plates for any person who cared to take one.

However, when Anisetta herself went up to thank him, he felt in a capacious side pocket of his jacket, and with his delicate, pale fingers, pulled out yet another passport. This he handed to Anisetta, saying:

"It's just the same as the other passport, but I thought you would like a spare one. It might come in useful if you lose the other one—or if you travel separately. Not," he added, blushing again at risking the pleasantry, "not that Aquila is likely to let you do *that*."

Anisetta laughed. She took the passport. She did not open it to see whether, in fact, it was the same. She knew that if Uncle Domenico said it was, then it was. He was the most reliable forger in Sicily. He was not actually a member of Giorgio's gang. He had his own business. But he and his brother were very friendly.

Just now Uncle Domenico was resting on his laurels. The laurels had been gained in the war, when the British gave him a special decoration. He had been employed in forging currency notes for parachutists. He had got the job with typical Morales savoir-faire. Already a forger of some fifteen years' standing when the Allies invaded Sicily, he had sent to Intelligence Headquarters an engraving of a man bending over a copperplate on which was in turn engraved a perfect replica of a hundred-lire note. He called it "The Old Counterfeiter." After several weeks the British Commanding Officer had, as he said, come to the point with Uncle Domenico bluntly.

An artist, said the officer, like Domenico had no business to be wasting his time doing fancy pictures even if this *was* Italy; not in time of war. There was a job to do. Uncle Domenico diffidently did it. He got a medal.

*   *   *

The guests passed Domenico's passports admiringly from hand to hand.

The mandolin orchestra struck a loud chord and the wedding-guests moved away from the middle of the room.

Aquila came forward, his hands outstretched towards Anisetta, his intelligent, fine-drawn young face (for he took after Uncle Domenico rather than his more famous uncle) beaming with pleasure.

"May I have the honor," he said to Anisetta, "of our first dance?"

It is a pleasant Sicilian custom that the bride performs her first dance with her husband while still wearing her wedding dress. Thus Anisetta, as her husband took her in his arms, looked so beautiful that many of the guests were moved to tears.

Aquila and Anisetta stepped slowly into a waltz.

"A handsome couple," said Uncle Domenico to Uncle Giorgio.

"They are indeed," said Uncle Giorgio. "Aquila takes after you for good looks."

"But after *you* for brains," said Uncle Domenico. "I never did have any myself. All I have is my gift."

"And a wonderful gift it is," said Uncle Giorgio.

They watched the bride and bridegroom dancing for a while.

Uncle Domenico gave a little sigh.

"I shall miss you, Giorgio. Do you think you will like England? You haven't been there before, have you?"

"No," said Uncle Giorgio. Then, after a pause: "I hear it's very clean."

"Very," agreed Uncle Domenico. "Aquila tells me that in England cleanliness is next to Godliness."

"Yes," said Uncle Giorgio, blowing down his pipe stem to clear it. "And God is next to nothing; from all I hear, that is."

"Really?" said Uncle Domenico. "I don't think I should like that. I wouldn't call myself a religious man, but I don't like to see sacred things ignored. I suppose it's the artist in me. A man with a gift can't help feeling that it comes from somewhere outside himself, if you see what I mean."

"I do," said Uncle Giorgio, and added. "Very proper."

"No," continued Uncle Domenico, "I don't really envy you. I shall be happier here in our own little Monte Tauro. 'Live in a place where you know all the faces,' that's my motto for a happy life."

"Mine too," said Giorgio. "For different reasons, of course. But still, I wanted to give Aquila a present after his own heart; and I shall have to go along with him to see that he comes to no harm."

The waltz finished and Anisetta flung her arms round her husband's neck and standing on tip-toe, kissed him.

"Well, there's one thing certain," said Uncle Domenico to Uncle Giorgio. "You'll have a happy pair as travelling companions."

But there Uncle Domenico was wrong. That very day Aquila and Anisetta had their first quarrel.

CHAPTER II

THE BACKWARD BRIDE

The trouble began when they were riding in a posse down the slopes of Mount Etna, on the first stage of their honeymoon.

The posse was made up of Aquila on a mule, Uncle Giorgio on a small undistinguished grey horse with very sure feet, twenty-seven brigands on twenty-seven different sorts of horses and mules with guns across their saddles, and in the middle of them all Anisetta, riding the very white horse that appeared in all the photographs of Orlando.

At first no one spoke because the path was very difficult. It twisted in and out of great cliffs of lava, leading through a landscape so forbidding as to make the traveller feel he was wayfaring in a part of Hell that had cooled and grown a crust over its fires.

Then the cavalcade turned a corner and rode suddenly into a great grove of olive trees. When they had come out of it the landscape before them had grown marvellously gentle; and far below them they could see the blue waters of the Ionian Sea.

When they had passed the last of the olive trees they came out upon a terrace on which grew vines. Orlando, who was leading, reined in his horse and with a fine and most brigandly gesture pointed down the mountain to where, at its feet, lay the port of Catania.

The brigands began singing a long sad song about Saint Lucy, and they all moved forward again, some of the brigands shifting their guns to a more handy position, for they were approaching the boundaries of Uncle Giorgio's brigand-kingdom.

9

In a few moments the mountain track became a road, and the whole cavalcade halted. This was the beginning of that part of Sicily which had been governed, in the last fifty years, by a king, a dictator, a German general, an American colonel, a British major, and finally a freely-elected Prime Minister: unlike the regions the bandits had just traversed, which had enjoyed the tranquillity of Uncle Giorgio's uninterrupted rule for more than two decades.

The brigands formed a circle.

Uncle Giorgio seized the bridle of Anisetta's horse and Aquila's mule. He led them into the middle of the circle.

The brigands raised their rifles and with a great shout of *Arrivederci!*, they fired a rattling farewell salute.

*   *   *

There are those sorts of people who think that firecrackers, rifles and so forth make a rather jolly noise: and there are those who do not. In the first category are all Chinese, all Indians and most Sicilians. In the second category was Aquila.

Anisetta clapped her hands, Uncle Giorgio's eyes glistened, but Aquila looked as glum as the mule on which he sat. And when in response to Anisetta's demand for more, the brigands let off a second volley, he screwed up his eyes, frowned, and his mouth took on a disapproving droop.

This was because he felt morally superior.

He was by no means the only person who has felt morally superior to someone else because he takes no joy in a loud bang and the other person does. The European deplores the Hindu when he lets off crackers in Divali, the American looks down upon the Italian when he explodes maroons on saints' days, and the Englishman only forgives the Arab for his festive musketry because he does it while riding a horse. Aquila forgave nobody. He thought that the brigands were behaving like savages. He was glad he was above it. And if it seems that he had a strange reason for feeling moral superiority, that should cause no thoughtful person surprise. All reasons for

feeling morally superior are strange, when you come to ex-
amine them.

Had it not been for the volley, Aquila would probably
have held his peace and thus postponed his quarrel with his
wife. But as it was, no sooner had the brigands cantered away
back into the mountains, than Aquila unburdened his mind of
a few points that had been troubling him.

Uncle Giorgio was riding slightly ahead. Aquila excused
himself to Anisetta and spurred his mount until it was ambling
beside that of the brigand.

"Uncle," said Aquila, pointing to where the town lay
below them, "we'll soon be coming into civilization, and then
my wonderful wedding present will really begin."

"Yes," said Uncle Giorgio.

"There's just one thing needed to make it perfect," said
Aquila.

"Then you shall have it, Aquila," said Uncle Giorgio.

"That's splendid!" said Aquila. "And it's really quite
simple. You see, thanks to your generosity I have been able
to move in the world outside Monte Tauro rather more than
you, Uncle, and—well, I mean, people don't look on brigands
quite as they used to; I mean—well what I mean is would you
mind very much if I, so to speak, took the lead on our trip
rather than you? I feel you might find things rather changed
since you were in New York. There's been a lot of Progress
in twenty years."

"Of course you may take the lead, my boy," said Uncle
Giorgio. "Why should you think that I would object? I *never*
want to take the lead. I always feel that there must be better
men to do it than me: and I confess I find it rather odd that
so often no one comes forward."

Men have extirpated religions, destroyed empires, usurped
thrones and massacred whole nations, with this same attitude
of mild surprise at the fact that nobody but themselves seemed
willing to take on the job. But young Aquila took it for true
modesty.

"That's settled then," said Aquila.

"Indeed, yes," said Giorgio. "You mustn't fall for this popular legend that I am a proud and domineering man. I've never domineered in my life. As for being proud, well, I must confess I'm a little proud of my marksmanship. It's not everybody who can bring a man down in one shot at seven hundred yards. But you know, even with that, it's remarkable how few times I've actually had to do it. People seem quite content to take my word for it."

"I hope," said Aquila decisively, "that you won't have to do it at all in the future. Not, at least, on our tour. In fact, I'd much prefer if you didn't draw your gun at all until we get back to Monte Tauro."

"I shall certainly do my best not to," said Uncle Giorgio earnestly. "It might be very difficult for you if I did. Socially, I mean."

"I'm glad you understand," said Aquila. "Thank you," and turning his mule he trotted back to his wife. He had another thing on his mind, and he felt in a persuasive mood. He fell in beside his wife and said, by way of preface:

"Enjoying yourself?"

"Um!" said Anisetta, who enjoyed most things. "Are you?"

"Well," said Aquila, "it's early yet. I shan't really begin to enjoy myself until I'm out of this backward island of ours. And, come to think of it, not even then. I shall not really be happy until I'm face to face with Professor Lissom himself."

"Oh, yes?" said Anisetta politely. "I suppose he must be a very interesting man."

"If only you would read his books," said Aquila disingenuously.

"Me?" said Anisetta in astonishment. "I've never read a book in my life, except the Bible and only that in ever so little bits."

"Oh, but Pina," said Aquila, even more disingenuously, "you'd find his *Morals for Moderns* just as easy to read as the Bible, and very much more progressive."

Anisetta at first took no more notice of this speech than did her white horse.

Then she gave a little start.

"Ooo!" she said, "you mean me, don't you? I can't get used to you calling me 'Pina.' It's my name, of course, but everybody has always called me Anisetta."

This, as Aquila knew, was because she had got illicitly drunk at the age of four on the popular liqueur of this name. The incident had been much enjoyed by everybody.

"I don't think Anisetta is a very sophisticated name," said Aquila, "and when we get out of Sicily we shall have to be sophisticated, like everybody else and stop being crude peasants."

"Why must we be phisticated?" asked Anisetta. "We were married in a church, weren't we, and that ought to be good enough for anybody."

Aquila looked at her in bewilderment for a moment. Then tumbling to her meaning, he said:

"My dear, being sophisticated isn't a ceremony. It's—well, it's being a lady."

Anisetta scratched her horse's neck for a while and then sighed.

"I don't think I really want to be a lady," she said at last. "What I want is to be a good wife and have twelve children."

"Twelve!" said Aquila with such violence that his mule slithered to a dead stop and laid back its ears.

By the time that Aquila had persuaded it to start again, he was once more in command of himself.

"But if only you would read Professor Lissom's books," he said to his wife, "or let me tell you what is in them, you would learn what a really modern marriage can be."

"Oh," said Anisetta with a bright smile, "so *that* is what you are driving at." She chuckled. "But you needn't have bothered. I know all about marriage because last night my mother told me all the facts of life."

Holding the reins with one hand, she proceeded to mark off the facts of life with the fingers of her other.

"I've got to love my husband . . ." she said.

"Right," said Aquila.

"Keep him well fed."

"Right," said Aquila.

"Nurse him when he's sick."

"Right," said Aquila but with some impatience.

"Send his children to church," said Anisetta.

"Maybe," said Aquila, openly restless.

"And not let him use self-control because I am a Catholic," concluded Anisetta triumphantly.

"Not *self*-control," said Aquila.

"That's what my mother said," replied Anisetta.

"Not *quite* what your mother said," Aquila corrected her.

"Yes, it was," said Anisetta, "and my mother ought to know because she had an awful time with father when they were first married. He wouldn't go to Sunday Mass at all."

Uncle Giorgio turned in his saddle to warn them that the road was becoming less of a road than a series of rough steps cut in the living marble of the hill. They nodded to each other, Aquila a little sharply because he was beginning to lose patience with Anisetta's obtuseness. But Anisetta smiled as gaily as a bride should.

Aquila's mule trod on a loose stone. Aquila bounced in his saddle and his teeth rattled in his head.

"You mean *birth*-control," said Aquila sharply. "It's not . . ."

His mule, unnerved by its first mistake, misjudged the smoothness of a piece of marble and it slid down the next three steps. Aquila bit his tongue.

Anisetta's white horse followed half a pace behind the mule, and followed so surely of foot that it was difficult not to believe that it was profiting by the mule's mistakes.

Anisetta, riding easily, turned Aquila's words over in her mind. She beamed.

"That's it!" she cried. "That's just what my mother *did*

say. I couldn't quite make it out at the time because she was fitting my wedding-dress and her mouth was full of pins. But you're quite right. It was birth-control and I mustn't do it because I'm a Catholic."

The road levelled out. Anisetta's horse came up beside Aquila.

"Look!" said Aquila sharply. "Let us not waste words. What I want you to do is to read an Italian translation of a book by Professor Lissom on just the subject which we have, in a rambling way, been trying to talk about. Now promise me you'll read it and follow his advice. Promise like a good wife and we'll say no more about it."

"I promise," said Anisetta.

Aquila was so pleased that if he had had his way he would have reined in his mount, leaned over and embraced his wife then and there. But he did not have his way, for the road broke into steps again and once more the mule found that its self-confidence had deserted it.

"That's fine," was all that Aquila could say to express his pleasure. A little later, above the clatter of hooves on the marble rocks, he added:

"I'm glad you're rising so quickly above your village up-bringing. This business of family limitation has worried me a good deal, I can assure you. I discussed it with some liberal-minded friends at Palermo University, but they advised me not to mention it to you until we were actually married. I explained, you see, that your mother was a dyed-in-the-wool reactionary. Still, it's all happily settled now."

"Yes," said Anisetta.

"There's a whole section on birth-control in Lissom's book: pretty frank, so people think. But it states the blunt facts. I want you to read it carefully."

"I shall," said Anisetta. "But it's not really necessary. Reading always gives me a headache and in any case I agree with the Professor. It's wicked."

"What do you mean, you 'agree with the Professor'?" said Aquila.

"Doesn't he think it's wicked?"

"Certainly not."

"Does he do it?"

"Of course he does."

"But," said Anisetta in great astonishment, "what does his priest say?"

They passed the first house they had seen close-to since they left Monte Tauro.

"My dear Pina," said Aquila, "Professor Lissom is an Englishman. In England they do not take their morals from a parish priest. They think for themselves. Remember that, Pina. *They think for themselves.* That is something quite new for you, I know, but it's something that I want you to get used to as soon as you possibly can. Now I am going to tell you something else you will find in Professor Lissom's famous book. Professor Lissom doesn't believe in marriage."

"You mean he's a bachelor," said Anisetta.

"On the contrary," Aquila replied, "he has been married three times. But he doesn't believe that marriage is necessary for modern men and women who want to make love to each other. He thinks that they should just . . . well . . . do you see what I mean?"

"I do," said Anisetta. But Aquila explained himself further because he was liberating Anisetta's mind from reactionary ideas and for this purpose, following the example of all progressive persons, he assumed that she had no mind at all. He therefore swept on:

"Professor Lissom believes that when a man wants to go to bed with a woman, he does not need to wait for a priest to give him a permit. After all, who is likely to know better what's good for him? Nature or a clergyman?"

Anisetta considered this.

"I follow you," she said at last. "You mean that Professor Lissom being an Englishman can't rely on a priest because all the priests there are Protestants. And who would trust a heretic?"

Aquila smiled indulgently. "In a limited way," he said,

"that is quite an intelligent observation. But try to see a little beyond your village notions. When I say that Professor Lissom prefers to trust his natural instincts rather than a priest, I mean any priest, even a Catholic one. Now think again: which is more likely to be right; Mother Nature, or a *Catholic* priest?"

This time Anisetta did not have to pause before she answered.

"The Catholic priest," she said decisively, "because he's got no natural instincts at all. It's like when Palermo plays Syracuse at football. They always have a referee from Catania because he doesn't give a toot on his whistle which side wins. He just sees to it that they stick to the rules."

"But what *are* the rules?" said Aquila, imitating Socrates.

"The Ten Commandments."

"But what are the Ten Commandments?"

Anisetta told him, without taking breath from the beginning of the first to the end of the tenth.

"I did not mean what *are* the Ten Commandments. I meant what *are* they," said Aquila.

"I've told you," said Anisetta. "I can say them backwards if you like. At least I think I can. I haven't done it since I went to Catechism classes. We used to do it to make the nuns mad at us."

"Professor Lissom says that the Ten Commandments," said Aquila, imperiously talking her down, "were a set of rules laid down by Moses to keep a lot of Jewish goat-herds in order."

"And goat-herds take some keeping in order, I can tell you," said Anisetta. "Look at the way they behave when they come into town for the cattle fairs. One drink, and no decent girl can show her face on the piazza."

"Very well," said Aquila, somewhat raising his voice, "they're good rules for goat-herds. I don't deny it. But they're not good enough for Professor Lissom. They're not good enough for millions of cultivated and intelligent people who do not, in their ordinary daily round, behave like goat-herds."

"Yes, I see that," said Anisetta, reasonably, "but even if they don't want to behave like goat-herds, that's no reason why they should want to behave like goats."

"What is the use of trying to explain anything to an ignorant pig-headed country bumpkin?" roared Aquila.

His mule stopped and stood with all four legs rigid, gazing at the side of the road. Aquila kicked its flanks.

"Don't kick him," said Anisetta. "It's that piece of white rag hanging on the cactus that has frightened him. Let him look at it quietly and tell him that it is only a piece of white rag."

"Mule," said Aquila between his teeth, "the object at which you are looking is only a piece of white rag."

The mule sighed windily and moved on.

"There!" said Anisetta. "Mules are very difficult creatures to handle, but I've always seemed to be good at it. But you were saying, Aquila . . . ?" she added politely.

Right and wrong are difficult enough to explain in any circumstances, but to explain them while inexpertly riding a mule is next to impossible. Aquila had to make things very simple.

"Look," he said, "it's like this. Professor Lissom believes that sex is the most powerful urge in man and that it mustn't be thwarted."

"So do goats," hissed Anisetta, "just you watch 'em."

"If you mention that animal again," shouted Aquila at the top of his voice, "I shall ride straight ahead and not speak to you again for forty-eight hours."

Uncle Giorgio turned round in his saddle.

"Are you two enjoying yourselves back there?" he called amiably. "Don't let me spoil it, but we're coming into a village, so if Aquila wants to take the lead here's as good a place as any. No hurry! Wait till we get to the statue of Sant'Agata by the roadside."

He waved his hand cheerily to them and faced ahead once more.

Aquila glared at Anisetta.

Anisetta hung her head.

"I am sorry I interrupted," she said. "I am very ignorant. Please go on."

"So you ought to be sorry," said Aquila, mopping his forehead.

"Well, now," he continued, "old-fashioned people thought that if a man and woman made love to each other without getting married it was shocking. But reasonable modern people in England and America and so on, like Professor Lissom, say, 'Supposing they can't get married: supposing they don't know if they like each other enough to get married: supposing that they're married already to two other persons. Does that mean that they've got to thwart their sexual impulses?' "

Anisetta opened her mouth to reply but Aquila refused to pause.

"The answer to my question," he went on, "is that they should live in what used to be called sin. Maybe that would shock your mother. But if we ran the world according to your mother's ideas we would still be in the Middle Ages. Fortunately, outside Sicily we don't. We run it according to Professor Lissom's. So now you see why we've got to revise the Ten Commandments. Well, *now* what do you say?"

Anisetta, who was riding side-saddle, turned with a graceful movement towards her husband.

"*I* should say," she answered, "that your Professor Lissom was fond of a bit of skirt. So was my father. He was a great one for the girls, was my father. He didn't believe in the Ten Commandments either. But my mother didn't revise the Bible. She revised father."

Aquila struck his forehead with his clenched fist.

The mule stopped; Aquila swore.

"That," he said to his mule with, for so young a man, a very bitter voice, "that object at which you are so stupidly staring, is a statue of Sant'Agata which is venerated by ignorant, narrow-minded, prejudiced and *talkative* young Sicilian girls who not only do not know any better but are determined not to learn. You may, with safety, pass it by!"

With that he drove his heels into his mule's flanks, the mule started forward in a wild gallop, and Aquila rode up to join his uncle without so much as another glance at his exasperating bride.

*   *   *

Anisetta rode on, feeling very ashamed. When Uncle Giorgio fell back beside her, she was too upset to say a word to him. When he pressed her to tell him what was wrong she finally said:

"I do not think I have been a good wife."

No doubt this was true. But she had been, on the other hand, a remarkably good prophet.

Professor Lissom *was* inordinately fond of a bit of skirt, as they all found out to their cost when the Greek sea-captain finally got them all to England.

CHAPTER III

REMINISCENCES OF A THOUGHTFUL BRIGAND

Uncle Giorgio told Aquila and Anisetta about the Greek captain as they were walking through the more obscure backstreets of Catania towards the port.

They had got rid of the horses and the mule. They had given them to an old woman who was married to a hackney carriage driver and who was the mother of Orlando. In spite of having so well-placed a son, the old woman still went out to work. She cleaned floors: but this does not reflect on Orlando's filial piety because the floors she cleaned were in the Catania Police Headquarters. As all the policemen said, she was one of the old school, she was not afraid of long hours and hard work. In fact, it was notorious that detective-inspectors coming out of a conference at midnight had found old mother Caterina on her hands and knees swabbing down the corridor. She might easily have been suspected of eavesdropping, but as everyone knew, she was stone-deaf.

Uncle Giorgio had ridden beneath her window and whistled the sad song about St. Lucy that the brigands had sung on the way down, and the old crone had promptly appeared.

Uncle Giorgio had then said a few words in a voice that was too low for Aquila to hear; the old woman had nodded, descended to the street door, and led away their horses.

A boy was found to carry Anisetta's box, and now made a fourth as the travellers walked towards the dock and Giorgio explained about the Greek.

"He is a captain who is under something of an obligation to me," said Uncle Giorgio. "His ship is not very large, but it

21

makes quite good speed. We should be in England in about a fortnight."

"Did you say he was a Greek?" asked Aquila.

"Yes," said Uncle Giorgio. "There are usually a few of them in port at this time of year. They come over from Athens in the olive-oil ships."

"Athens!" exclaimed Aquila. "A Greek from Athens. In fact, an Athenian!"

"Oh, but I think that in this case it will be all right," said Uncle Giorgio. "All Athenians are not necessarily crooked, although I grant you that it is safer to assume that they are. In dealing with Greeks, everything depends on whether they think they can browbeat you into paying a handsome advance. If you do, you're lost. But if you put up a firm front and don't even show them a sight of your money until the job is finished, they are generally quite honest. Now this captain, for instance . . ."

"You misunderstand me," said Aquila. "In calling your captain an Athenian I was not concerned with his honesty; I was concerned with his glorious past."

"I would call it lurid rather than glorious," said Giorgio. "But of course it depends on one's point of view. For instance, running a ship on the rocks while drunk would be nothing against, for instance, a poet. But for a sea-captain . . ."

"You misunderstand me again," said Aquila. "When I refer to the captain's past I do not mean his personal history but that of Plato, of Aristotle, of Sophocles and even," he said with a vivid touch, "our own Archimedes, who may have walked these very streets."

"These?" said Anisetta, but not because she doubted the statement. On the contrary, she had no reason to suppose that Archimedes did not walk the streets of Catania, since she had not the least idea who he was. But she wanted to show a bright interest in her husband's conversation.

"These," answered Aquila, shortly, because he was still angry with her. To Uncle Giorgio he went on to give an outline of the great history of the Greeks and their part in Eu-

rope's culture. By the time he had, with Aeneas, left Dido
and was founding Rome, they came in sight of the harbor.

Rome's struggle with Hannibal and her spiritual conquest
by the Greeks brought them to the quayside. The early history
of the Byzantine Empire brought them in sight of a small ship.
There, as is the way with so many other historians, Aquila
broke off his narrative.

He looked at the ship. He looked at Uncle Giorgio. Uncle
Giorgio cleared his throat.

"It's like small boys," he said. "Just as no ordinary human
is ever quite as dirty as a small boy, so no ship is ever quite
as dirty as a small ship."

Aquila examined the tramp-steamer from the gear that
fell in festoons of tangles from the mainmast, past the rusty
bridge, the dented smoke-stack and an unnamable erection of
corrugated iron behind it, past the heap of litter aft, to the
Greek characters, once white, of her name. It was a far cry
from the Parthenon.

Uncle Giorgio cleared his throat a second time.

"She's inconspicuous, at any rate," he said apologetically.

"To us, no doubt," said Aquila. "But the dustbin outside
what I take to be the captain's cabin might, to a seamanly
eye, serve to pick her out."

"You are always surprising me with the range of the things
you know," said Giorgio, very pleasantly. "I would never have
guessed that that was the captain's cabin, but you are quite
right: it is. There is the captain himself."

"Where?" said Aquila incredulously.

"At the cabin door, putting something in the dustbin,"
replied Giorgio.

To Aquila, as to most well-educated young men, the word
"Greek" conjured up bearded philosophers and straight-nosed
youths walking to and from the gymnasium deep in moral
conversation.

They boarded the ship. The captain, wheezing and grunt-
ing, came to meet them.

He was a vast man with a fleshy nose that formed no more

than a prominent billow in the folds of fat that made up his face. His hands were as fleshy as his nose; his ears were fleshy, his lips were fleshy and when he coughed he thudded like a chopper hitting a joint of meat. In a moment it was clear to Aquila that if this particular Greek walked to and from the gymnasium he certainly never went inside.

Uncle Giorgio spoke to the Greek in English. He answered briefly in the same language but with difficulty. He rolled to the side of his ship to see if the three had been followed. Finding they had not, he beckoned them towards his own cabin. It had four bunks.

"You," he said, and wheezed with the utmost amiability at all of them. "Me go. For you."

Uncle Giorgio indicated Anisetta and Aquila.

"I'm afraid my agent could not have made himself clear," he said. "This young lady and gentlemen are—. I don't think, that is, that a four berth cabin would quite suit their—I mean —our purpose."

The captain looked at him uncomprehendingly.

Giorgio seized Anisetta by the arm, and pulled her forward.

"Look," he said. "This is why Aquila," and he pointed to his nephew, "will need a separate cabin. Altro. Other. Two. Due," he said.

The captain looked. The captain turned to Aquila; the captain, with the sound of hitting a side of beef, hit his thigh; the captain spoke to Aquila in English:

"Fee Mean," he said, and winked in the deep recesses of his face. "Fee Mean! Hoo hoo hoo! Fee Mean eh?" and he poked Aquila in the ribs.

He meant 'Women.' There was no doubt about it. Aquila, indeed, wished passionately that there were. But the captain's winks, leers, gestures and nudges in Aquila's ribs left no room for mistaking his meaning. He meant 'Women' and he kept saying it:

"Fee Mean! Hoo, ha. Fee Mean eh? Hoo!"

With that he waddled off down a companionway, beckoning with his sausage-fingers for them to follow.

Aquila found it difficult to keep back his tears. It was a bitterly disappointing start to his holiday. If only, he said to himself, he had not been a Greek. The rest he could have forgiven, but he could never forgive him for being a compatriot of Phidias and Plato.

With the thought of those two names, his tears would not be denied. Observing them, Uncle Giorgio laid a kindly hand upon his arm and said:

"Do not be disappointed, Aquila. He is a rough man and lacks education. Why, he is not even a captain. Your relative Domenico forged his master's ticket."

"Then," said Aquila, drying his eyes, "if he is a charlatan, perhaps he is not even a Greek."

"I'm sure that if he is, he ought to be ashamed of himself," said Uncle Giorgio soothingly. "If Hannibal had met the captain he would have been most disapproving."

"Yes, I see what you mean, Uncle," said Aquila. He blew his nose. "But Hannibal was not a Greek. He was a Carthaginian."

"How stupid of me," said Giorgio. "Of course he was. Well then, say Dido."

"She was a Carthaginian, too."

"It is remarkable," said Uncle Giorgio stiffly, "how many famous Greeks chose to live in Carthage. They must have preferred the climate. Anyway, Dido was a remarkable woman of the finest discrimination, and she would have detested the captain. And talking of remarkable women, perhaps you had better take Anisetta to your cabin. She must be very tired."

"Of course," said Aquila and gave her his arm. As they came to the top of the companion-way, he turned back to Giorgio and said:

"Thank you, Uncle."

Giorgio, in a graceful Sicilian phrase, blessed their wedding night and then tactfully withdrew behind a ventilator to spare their embarrassment.

There was no tact about the captain. He flung open the door of the cabin with a rollicking barrage of chuckles. He

patted the two bunks that were fixed in the wall one above
the other, as though he were anxious that by no oversight of
his would they mistake them for anything but beds. When
Anisetta's box was brought in, he shook with such laughter
that the box might have been a circus clown. And finally, as
he stood in the door, he blew Anisetta a suety kiss.

With that he sighed, shook his head, smiled, and closing
the door, said:

"Fee Mean. Hoo, hoo, hoo!"

*   *   *

At about ten o'clock the same night, the ship being still
tied up to the quay, Aquila and Anisetta retired to their cabin,
leaving Giorgio to smoke a last pipe on deck.

They closed the door. They looked at the bunks.

"Well," said Anisetta, and fell silent.

"Well," said Aquila, and fell silent in his turn.

At length Anisetta said:

"Well, we're married."

At which Aquila said:

"Why, yes, we are."

"I suppose then," said Anisetta, "I had better undress."

*   *   *

At about eleven o'clock that night, Anisetta, dressed in a
night shift and dressing-gown, stormed down the deck of the
tramp-ship, viciously kicking rubbish out of her path, and
calling for Uncle Giorgio.

She found him sitting on a pile of tangled rope. He was
smoking his pipe and admiring the snow on the top of Mount
Etna as it glimmered in the starlight.

Anisetta flung herself down beside him.

"He is mad," she said.

Uncle Giorgio looked at her, but said nothing.

"As his wife I am sorry to say it, but he's a lunatic," said
Anisetta.

"You mean Aquila?" said Giorgio.

"I do."

"Why?" asked Giorgio.

"Because he will not go to bed with me," said Anisetta.

"Oh," said Giorgio. "I see. Well, that has been known to happen before. The solution is very simple."

"What is it?"

"*You* must go to bed with *him*," said Giorgio.

"I've tried that," said Anisetta. "He is in the top bunk and he was reading a notice, so I climbed up and hung on to the rail and said, 'What are you reading, Aquila?' And he said, 'I am reading the notice which tells you how to put on a life-belt if the ship goes down.' So I climbed into his bunk and said, 'Ooo how interesting, let me see,' then he said, 'You have one exactly the same posted at the head of your own bunk.' So you see, Uncle, it is no good. He will not go to bed with me because I will not use birth-control. He says he wants a rational marriage. He says he doesn't want his son to be born a backward Sicilian, either. He wants him to be born in a progressive country but hasn't quite made up his mind which. Uncle, do all wives think their husbands crazy?"

"No, my dear, not all," said Uncle Giorgio. "Only those who take the trouble to listen when their husbands are talking."

"But Uncle Giorgio, Aquila *is* crazy. It is not just that I feel that he is. He thinks and reasons and argues all the time about our baby. You cannot have babies by thinking."

"You cannot do anything that is really important by thinking," Uncle Giorgio agreed. "All women know that, even a very young one like you."

"Yes," said Anisetta.

"That is why women are weak," said Uncle Giorgio.

"Why?"

"Because they are frightened, and quite rightly too. They know that all the great and important things in their lives— like falling in love, having children, being fond of those children beyond all common sense—these things happen without thinking. They just happen, Anisetta, and not the cleverest

person in the world can stop them. Clever people can argue
them away when they have happened. But they cannot stop
them happening. *You* know, Anisetta, but Aquila does not,
that we are not responsible for our actions. Who, knowing
that, wouldn't be afraid?"

"Is Aquila afraid?"

"No."

"But why not, Uncle? I am. You are quite right. I am
very much afraid. Why isn't Aquila?

"Because he is a man, my dear. And you are a woman."

"But are you afraid, Uncle?"

"Yes, my dear."

"But nobody would call you a woman, Uncle. At least not
to your face, and live."

"That is the whole reason, Anisetta. You see, in my profession you many times have men's lives at your mercy. I myself
have often held my knife to a man's throat. One single movement of my wrist"—Uncle Giorgio neatly demonstrated with
his pipe—"and the man is dead."

Anisetta gave a delighted little shudder. It was not every
Sicilian girl who had married into a bandit's family.

"And then again," said Uncle Giorgio, "I could let him
live. I could, you see, bring a new life into the world simply
by moving my hand away; because it was a new life that I
could give him, he being as good as dead."

"Which did you do, Uncle?"

"Whatever I did, my dear, I always knew one thing. . . .
I had not the slightest idea why I did it. No more than you
will know when you have brought Aquila's son into the world.
So you see, in a strange way, I am very like a woman."

"But Uncle, everybody in Sicily knows that you are a very
just brigand. You only kill bad men. You let the good ones
live. So you must know what you are doing when you do it."

"Is that what they say about me, my dear?"

"Yes, everybody."

"Nobody would say that, Anisetta," said Uncle Giorgio,

"who had ever given a man his life and then seen what he has done with it. I have. A very long time ago, when I was young, a man pleaded on his bended knees to me not to kill him. He told me of his love for his wife and his care for his children: he told me of the charitable works he had done and swore to do in future; he told me how he went to Mass every Sunday and of the new altar cloth he had just bought and paid for and given to the Cathedral. He told me how good he was to his workmen and how he looked after their children when they fell sick. He told me his philosophy of life and it was very like a modest version of the Sermon on the Mount. Strange as it may seem, my fellow brigands bore him out in every word he said. More: even their wives agreed he was telling the truth. So I did not kill him. I blindfolded his eyes, led him away from our headquarters by a roundabout road, and I let him go."

"Ooo!" said Anisetta, clapping her hands, "what a wonderful story. May I tell it to my son? I want him to be very very proud of his famous uncle."

"Yes," said Giorgio, "you may. As long as you promise me you will always tell him the end of it."

"I promise. What is it, Uncle?"

"Ten years later I shot him dead in his tracks on my own mountain."

Anisetta's eyes grew round.

"Why, Uncle?"

"My dear," said Uncle Giorgio with a little grin, "he had been so impressed with what he had seen and heard at my headquarters that he turned brigand himself; and a very clever brigand too. In fact, twenty villages from round about sent a formal deputation to me insisting that since I had failed to shoot him once, it was my public duty to retrieve my error and rid the neighborhood of one of the biggest scourges it had ever suffered under. It was a fair request. I took my gun and went in search of him that very hour. I had made one mistake. I took care that I did not make another. In fact," he said, squinting one eye as though he were looking along a rifle barrel, "at seven hundred yards and with not too tricky a cross wind, I may say that I never do."

"That was the Bloody Bishop, wasn't it?" said Anisetta, proud to have identified the man in her uncle's story.

"Yes, my dear. But he wasn't a bishop really. He just talked like one."

Anisetta put her hand behind her head and leaned back against a stanchion.

"When my son becomes a brigand I won't want him to talk like the Bloody Bishop. I want him to talk like you," she said.

"No," said Giorgio, with a touch of the pedagogue. "You have got it wrong. It would be an excellent thing if he talked like the Bloody Bishop. But he should *shoot* like me."

"Uncle," said Anisetta, "I love you. And what you mean to say all the time is that it doesn't matter a bit how we have our baby or when."

"But it does," said Giorgio.

"Why?"

"Because your husband says it does."

"But just because a young man marries a woman it doesn't mean that from then on everything he says to her is wise and right and good and true."

"No. But he thinks it does."

"Well, I shall soon tell him different."

"No you won't, my dear. You'll flatter him into thinking that he's the wisest man who ever lived, because you know perfectly well that if you don't, he will go straight off and fall in love with some wicked woman who will."

She put a shapely hand upon Uncle Giorgio's knee, and solemnly nodded her head.

"You are quite right, Uncle," she said. "You always are quite right. Some women will stop at nothing to get a man. I've seen them. They'll lie and lie and lie and lie to a man till they get what they want. And then what happens? They leave him flat."

"Whereas you, my good little wife," said Uncle Giorgio

patting her hand, "will lie and lie and lie and lie for the rest of your life."

"Yes," she said stoutly.

Uncle Giorgio kissed the top of her head.

"We Morales are going to be proud of you," he said.

"Yes, Uncle, but you must help me. I must understand at least a little of what he is talking about. When he starts speaking it is no good my just staring at him with big loving eyes. You must help me to be intelligent about his plans for our son." She paused. "Well," she said, "not perhaps *be* intelligent; but look as though I am. For instance, he doesn't want our baby to be born a Sicilian. He wants to travel round and find a more progressive country. What do I say?"

"You say, 'How very wise.'"

"Is it?" asked Anisetta.

"No," said Giorgio, "but you must never say so. It is the sign of a great man to admit that he is wrong: but it is the sign of a saint to admit that his wife is right. No. You must agree with him and help him. You must learn all you can about the Americans and English and the French and the Spaniards until you know enough to be able to choose wisely and well. You must ask everybody questions."

Anisetta said:

"What will the Americans say when we ask them questions?"

Giorgio replied:

"They will say that Americans have their faults but they are valiant, kind, shrewd, reasonable, just, truthful and modest."

"Just like the Sicilians. And what will the Englishmen say?"

"They will say that the English have their faults, as none know better than the English, but on the whole they are valiant, kind, shrewd, reasonable, just, truthful and modest."

"Oh. And the French?"

"They will answer differently. They will not admit to having any bad traits, but only bad politicians. Apart from that they will prove to you that they are valiant, kind, shrewd, reasonable, just, truthful and modest."

Anisetta giggled and pinched her uncle's ear.

"Suppose, you wicked uncle," she said, "that we ask the King of the Cannibal Islands, just for the sake of a little variety." And she poised her fingers again over his ear.

"The King of the Cannibal Islands," said Giorgio, chuckling as he moved his ear out of danger, "will lean over the cooking-pot and tell you that his people are valiant, kind, shrewd, reasonable, just, truthful and modest, and that they owe this to living on a scientifically balanced diet. Then he will clap down the lid on your head . . . and serve you jolly well right for making fun of your uncle."

"Thank you, Uncle, and you know I wouldn't dream of making fun of you," said Anisetta. She got up and stretched herself like a cat. She looked at the snows on the mountain.

"So I was right after all. Aquila is crazy and our son might just as well be born in Sicily. Because if he is, then he will be all the things that you mentioned, and be born in the most beautiful place in the world."

Uncle Giorgio re-lit his pipe with care.

"At any rate," he said, "he'll have a most beautiful mother."

She smiled at the compliment but stuck to the point:

"What is the use of being beautiful if your husband will not go to bed with you?" she asked. Then she added, in a justly aggrieved voice: "On your wedding night too; and what's even more, on board a ship. I always thought that everybody on board a ship always went straight to bed with everybody else. Don't they?"

Giorgio considered the matter silently for a while.

"Yes," he said, "from my experience they do. But only when the ship is under way."

"Ah!" said Anisetta, "so *that's* it."

"Very probably," said Giorgio.

Next she asked:

"When do we sail?"

"At six."

Anisetta sighed.

"Tomorrow night won't be the same thing, but I suppose it can't be helped," she said. "Thank you, Uncle, and goodnight."

She went below. Without turning on the light she crept into her bunk and lay very still lest she should wake her husband. But Aquila did not wake or even stir in his sleep. Aquila was very fond, as we have seen, of giving people good advice: and such people always have a clear conscience, marvellous as that may seem. Aquila therefore slept soundly until the morning.

*   *   *

Next morning found the Greek captain on the bridge, steering his ship down the Straits of Messina.

He was not at his best. He never was at his best when in charge of a ship, but this particular morning he had more to contend with than navigation.

The night before, unable to sleep after seeing Giorgio and the bridal couple safely in their cabins, he had gone ashore.

Though it was late at night, a friend of his called Rosa, on whom he called by chance, was still receiving visitors. One of these the captain had knocked down. Shortly afterwards the captain himself had been knocked down, but by someone unknown. His only clear memory of the incident was of his friend Rosa hiding in a wardrobe and saying, as he fought, 'Not here! Not here!'

The captain remembered reflecting (after he had been knocked down and while he was being revived) that this remark was the apex of foolishness. Even this morning it still made him cross. Clearly, for such a fight on such a subject, there could have been no other place.

The captain passed his hand over his aching forehead. He peered ahead, and although the morning air was pellucid down the whole length of the Straits, it was not so for him. He switched on his clear-vision screen, but it belied its name.

He heard gay whistling from below.

"Good morning," said a cheerful young voice.

The captain looked over the rail. He saw Aquila, and grunted.

Aquila, taking this for an invitation, clambered up to the bridge.

"It is wonderful to think, captain," he said, airing his English, "that these are the very seas through which Ulysses steered his frail craft. Just behind us is the place where he met and defeated the renowned giant Polyphemus, and just in front of us is where the sirens sang. Perhaps it was there in the very patch of sea off our port bow," said Aquila, pointing, "that he stuffed the ears of the rowers with wax and tied himself to the mast."

Aquila glanced at the captain to see what effect this glimpse of his own cultural heritage was having on him. But behind the folds of his face, the Greek's expression was inscrutable.

"Yes," said Aquila, to heighten the drama, "perhaps we are following in his very tracks."

The captain turned and looked sceptically at the series of foaming zig-zags that streamed from their rudder. Aquila looked too.

"Well," said Aquila, "more or less."

The captain nodded.

"Some pedants are prepared to argue that the voyage took place in the Euxine sea."

The captain silently conveyed that he was not one of them.

"But never-dying legends say that it was here," said Aquila waving his hand at the view with a gesture as fine as the scenery.

The captain looked. The captain nodded.

"Sirens," he said hoarsely, "is 'orrible. They maka me jump."

"Not those sort of sirens," said Aquila. "I mean those mysterious females who led men to their rocky coasts with singing."

"Oh," said the captain, his face lighting up, "Fee Mean."

"Yes," said Aquila, with a certain amount of disgust. "Women."

"Over there?" said the captain, nodding his head in the direction of the Sicilian shore.

"Over there," agreed Aquila.

The captain sucked his teeth appreciatively. He looked at Aquila with a new interest.

"Yes," said Aquila thoughtfully. "It might be that they lived in the caves of those rocks for which we are now headed."

The captain looked, winced, and bawled at the quartermaster in a desperate effort to make Aquila's description less literally true.

Five minutes later, much shaken, the captain mopped his forehead and the valleys in his neck and cheeks.

"Now, far beyond this point," said Aquila, when order had been restored, "lie Scylla and Charybdis, said by some to be whirlpools, by others . . ."

He got no further.

"Go down below and eat you dam' breakfast," the captain bellowed at him, "or by gar I clap you one two bloody quick in the brig."

Aquila did not know what the brig was but he knew when he was not wanted. Feeling very hurt, he went below.

One hour later a storm blew up. Aquila was sea-sick on the spot, and stayed sick for many days following. Thus, although the boat was under way the marriage was not, and Anisetta, though not as sick as Aquila, was even more miserable.

CHAPTER IV

BEDROOM SCENE

Aquila did not properly recover until he had been two days in England, by which time they had arrived at Oxford.

In Oxford everybody knew Professor Lissom and Lissom, they discovered, was willing to know anybody because he was a popular broadcaster.

They went to his rooms and found a lively man of fifty with a sharp curved nose, hair that was only slightly grey and a pair of very inquisitive eyes.

He shook hands with Giorgio courteously: with Aquila warmly (when Aquila mentioned the radio); and with Anisetta slowly, gently and for a very long time.

When Giorgio said they came from Sicily, the great man was polite: when Aquila said that Lissom was his hero, he was affable. But when Anisetta merely said "T'ank you" for some coffee, he showered them all with a week of invitations on the spot.

The next few days were most successful. Professor Lissom gave Aquila an introduction to the leading undergraduates; he gave Uncle Giorgio an introduction to a Professor of Political Theory; and to Anisetta he gave his undivided attention.

Aquila was very happy because he found that the undergraduates at Oxford were even more serious-minded than he was: Uncle Giorgio was very happy because the Professor of Political Theory agreed that Giorgio's principle of robbing the rich and giving to the poor was quite the latest thing in theories; but Anisetta was not happy at all because she was a

36

good girl and a married woman, and she thought Professor Lissom a very peculiar gentleman.

Besides, Aquila would still not go to bed with her in case they should have a baby.

One night in their hotel bedroom Anisetta was sitting up in her twin-bed brushing her hair.

Aquila was sitting up in *his* twin-bed reading with bated breath a history of the Trade-Union martyrs of Tolpuddle. It was the story of how seven men in the last century were condemned to transportation to Australia for daring to form a combination of workers. The undergraduates had told Aquila it was an enthralling book. The bookseller at Mr. Blackwell's shop had assured him that all England was reading it and all Englishmen had agreed that it must not happen again because (as some said) it was a social injustice or because (as others maintained) Australia was now unfortunately a self-governing Dominion.

Aquila found the story so absorbing that he took no notice of his wife at all, save to give her, as Progressiveness demanded, a short summary of the plot. That done, he fell to reading again.

Anisetta watched her husband for a while. Then she said: "Aquila!"

"Yes, my dear?" said Aquila, still reading.

"While you were buying books this afternoon," said Anisetta, "Professor Lissom showed me the sights. Then we had tea at Fuller's. We had cream cakes."

Aquila closed his book, a forefinger marking his place.

"That was very kind of Professor Lissom," said Aquila. "I hope you insisted on paying your share. In England women are expected to do that when moving in advanced circles."

He opened his book again and went on reading. After a while Anisetta said:

"Aquila!"

Aquila gave a little sigh.

"Yes, my dear," he said.

"Professor Lissom had a long talk with me last night."

"I know," said Aquila. "He told me about it. He said that he discussed Greek philosophy with you. I think that you are a very lucky girl."

"We *began* by talking about philosophy," said Anisetta meaningfully. "But then he rambled."

"Such a pity I missed it all," said Aquila, shaking his head. "But one cannot be in two places at once. Professor Lissom was most keen for me to see the moon rise over Magdalen." He searched for a moment among the pile of new books on his bedside table, selected one, and held it up for Anisetta to see. "Here is a book which tells how Professor Lissom meets Plato in the Elysian fields and they have a most brilliant dialogue. I haven't read it yet but it just shows you how highly the English think of him."

Anisetta stopped brushing her hair for a moment to ask:

"In what fields?"

"Elysian," said Aquila stroking the glossy cover of the new book.

"I don't think he mentioned those to me," said Anisetta. "But he did say that there were lots of quiet country spots around Oxford that he would like to take me to. Whom did you say he met?"

"Plato."

"That same Greek that Lissom mentioned? The one who thinks that love ought to go no further than giving good advice to little boys?"

"Yes," said Aquila, absently skimming the book.

Anisetta brushed her hair a moment in silence, and then said:

"When they meet I don't think they'll see eye to eye."

Seeing that Aquila did not answer her, she laid aside her hair-brush, and tackled the subject that was on her mind more directly.

"Professor Lissom's got some awfully funny ideas on what's right and what's wrong, hasn't he?" she said.

Aquila smiled at her. He said, but in a kindly fashion:

"I dare say, my dear, that if you had met Copernicus you

would have sat up in bed afterwards telling me that he had some awfully funny ideas about the solar system."

"No, I wouldn't," said Anisetta with decision. "Copernicus or whatever his name is wouldn't be such a fool as to talk about the solar system to a girl like me. Five minutes with me and he'd know he was wasting his time. But Professor Lissom's ideas are the sort that any girl in Monte Tauro could understand." She paused. "I'm sorry to say," she added, primly, as became a married woman.

"Professor Lissom has a wonderful gift for explaining the most complicated ideas in an easily understood manner," said Aquila, quoting from the jacket of the book.

"I should just say he has," said Anisetta. But Aquila ignored her and getting out of bed, turned off the central light. He adjusted his reading lamp, climbed back into bed, and said:

"Now do go to sleep like a good little wife, Anisetta. I really must do some studying, and if you chatter so, I cannot concentrate."

Anisetta pouted, thumped her pillow, and flung herself down in the bed so hard the bed-springs sang.

She shut her eyes but she did not go to sleep. No woman alone with a man reading a book seriously believes that he is taking in a word of what is in front of him. She believes that he is actually waging a terrible internal war to keep down thoughts of physical passion. After a while they are moved, by pity, to say something.

Thus, Anisetta:

"Aq-uee-la darling."

Aquila sighed and frowned into his book.

"Aquila," persisted Anisetta, talking half through her pillow. "Suppose all this progress you're studying is wrong. Suppose we were just meant to say our Pater Noster and be as God made us."

Aquila groaned and shut his book with a clap.

He spoke very crossly:

"Anisetta! If you really want to stop me reading you do not have to call in the help of Almighty God. You merely have to tell me to turn off the light." And after throwing his book, noisily on the bedside-table, that is what he did.

Anisetta lay very still in the darkness.

Aquila rolled about in his bed for a while as though it were an unquiet grave, and at last he, too, was still.

For a while he lay deaf to anything but his own angry thoughts. Then he began to listen. He held his breath to listen better. He said:

"Anisetta."

Anisetta made a tiny noise.

"Anisetta, are you crying?"

"No," she sobbed.

No man is proof against tears, not even the most rational man. A saint weeping for his own shortcomings or a woman weeping for those of her husband must be appeased; the saint with a crown of glory, the woman with a kiss. Aquila got out of bed, crossed the room and kissed her. He sat on her bed and felt for her hand.

Anisetta stopped crying. She looked up at her husband and fondly studied his shape against the faint light coming through the window.

"I'm all right now," said Anisetta. She sniffed and squeezed his hand. "Quite all right," she said, and her voice quavered.

"Of course you are," said Aquila, in the ringing tones of a ship's doctor. "It's homesickness, that's all."

Anisetta said, "I could kick you." But this was not true, because when she tried her foot got tangled in a loose sheet.

She lost her temper.

"Why the blazes don't you get into the bed and make love to me?" she demanded furiously.

It is surprising how often that tender and romantic request is made, in real life, furiously: although one would never guess it from books.

"Because you will not take proper precautions," said Aquila calmly. "And far be it from me to force anyone to do what they do not want to do."

"Damn and blast your far-be-its," said Anisetta. "Look!"
she said and springing out of bed she put on the light and took
off her nightgown. "Did any of your Tolpuddle martyrs look
like that?"

Pedantry came to Aquila's aid at a critical moment.

"My dear," he said, "the Tolpuddle martyrs were all
men."

"Well did their wives look like me?" said Anisetta. "You
don't have to tell me. I know they didn't, otherwise their husbands would have stayed at home instead of making combina-
tions."

Aquila rose and took her in his arms.

"Pina, my sweet, you are dazzlingly beautiful and I do very
much want to make love to you."

He released her and sat on his own bed.

"But you see the human soul is like a chariot that is pulled
by two horses and reason is the charioteer that holds the reins.
There is one white horse that is nice and quiet and gentle, and
one black horse that is always straining at the bit in order to
indulge the pleasures of the senses."

"Oh!" gasped Anisetta. "Oh! How dare you! How dare
you call me a horse."

"I did *not* call you a horse," said Aquila.

"You did."

"I did not."

"You did. You called me a horse. Your own wife. A black
horse. Why don't you call me a sow?" she demanded at the
top of her voice.

"Because I don't want to call you a sow," said Aquila.

"Yes, you do."

"No, I don't."

"Oh, yes, you do. Go ahead!" she shouted, stamping her
foot. "*I* don't mind."

"For heaven's sake," whispered Aquila, "lower your voice
or you'll wake the whole hotel. I was not calling you names. I
was just telling you how Plato describes the human soul."

"If you mention that bloody Greek schoolmaster to me again," screamed Anisetta, "I shall smack your face."

*   *   *

At first blush there is nothing that is strong enough to halt a quarrel between husband and wife such as this, so deep a swathe does it cut in the personalities, the prides, the self-esteems of both partners. Nothing, it would seem, could be sufficiently important to bring the deadly conflict to an end.

In practice it was stopped by the man in the next room throwing a boot at the wall.

Immediately Aquila and Anisetta both fell silent and with a look of intense guilt crept to their respective beds. And yet, as is well known, a quarrel between two old gentlemen over a borrowed book has been known to survive an earthquake.

But if Anisetta had stopped quarreling, she had started thinking: and as she lay in bed, her back turned ostentatiously towards her disobliging husband, she formed a plan. She determined that nothing should stop her from being a good wife and having a successful marriage. If Aquila wanted her to be sophisticated, then sophisticated she would be: but in her own way.

*   *   *

Aquila woke at half-past seven. He yawned, rubbed his eyes, and turned with a pleasurable feeling of expectation to the books at his bedside table. He determined to put in half an hour with the Tolpuddle martyrs before breakfast.

But the book was not in its place. Instead, weighted down with a hair-brush, there was a sheet of paper. On it, written in large, straggling letters was this message.

"HAVE GONE TO LIVE IN SIN FOR A WEEK WITH PROFESSOR LISSOM BACK TUESDAY LUNCH

YOUR LOVING WIFE
A"

*   *   *

"Jealousy," said Aquila for the tenth time that day, and gulping his fifteenth cup of black coffee, "went out with Queen Victoria."

Uncle Giorgio, leaning back in one of the hotel lounge chairs, nodded. He nodded not from agreement, but from policy. He had found out, from a long experience that when young men are either drunk or deceived by a woman, they are omniscient. Therefore he always agreed that women were all the same; and he always agreed that it was not the drink but something the young man had eaten. Thus he usually achieved his object, which was, benignly, the same in both cases—to get the young man back to bed.

"Quite," said Uncle Giorgio.

"A rational, thinking man with a sense of dignity is never jealous. He cannot afford to be. What, after all, is more ridiculous than a cuckold?"

"Nothing that I can think of," said Uncle Giorgio.

Aquila drank off his coffee. He stared abstractedly into his cup.

"What did you say?" he asked suddenly.

"I said I could think of nothing more absurd than a cuckold."

"Don't be silly," said Aquila sharply, "there must be dozens of things."

"Come to think of it, I suppose there must be," said Uncle Giorgio agreeably.

"Of course there are. Besides, whoever mentioned such a stupid old-fashioned word anyway? Nowadays there are no such things as cuckolds."

"Naturally not," said Uncle Giorgio. Then, after a pause: "By the way, what *do* they call them nowadays?"

Aquila thought for a moment and then dismissed the matter impatiently:

"The subject simply isn't discussed. Not in polite society."

"Not in *very* polite society," agreed Uncle Giorgio, and then added, apologetically, "so I am told, that is."

"But what distinguishes a man from a beast?" asked Aquila.

"Precious little," said Uncle Giorgio, shaking his head more from a desire for a change of motion than from sorrow. But he saw that he had said the wrong thing. "I beg your pardon: *what* distinguishes men from beasts?"

"Reason!" said Aquila. "Reason, reason and again reason. When a man's wife goes away with another man, instinct says, 'Be jealous! Be angry! Fetch her back!' But reason says, 'Be calm: consider: control yourself: face facts.'

"And reason's right, I'm glad to say," said Uncle Giorgio. "Obviously the woman thinks the other man is a whole lot handsomer, wiser and kinder. So she goes to him. And that's that. Ah!" said Uncle Giorgio, "reason all the time, I always say. That's the stuff. Who would want to behave like animals?"

"Women," said Aquila promptly. "And that is where your theory is wrong. Women do not think the other man is wiser. They do not think he is kinder and they do not," said Aquila thumping the table, "think he is handsomer. Women, especially Sicilian women, are guided almost entirely by their instincts. It is men who are reasonable. Reason does not say, 'That's that,' in your fatalistic Sicilian way. Reason says that if you try to forbid a woman doing something on which she has set her heart, not only will you merely egg her on to do that very thing, but the results may also be disastrous. It is all very beautifully set out in a study of women's sexual urges which I have read but for the moment I cannot recall the name of the book."

"Genesis," said Uncle Giorgio with a helpful expression. "The third chapter."

"I was speaking of psychoanalysis," said Aquila coldly. "It is all too easy to produce in a woman a whole series of repressions, frustrations, inhibitions and what are crudely called complexes, until she lives in a constant state of nervous tension. It was all very well for the cave-man to hit his wandering wife over the head with a club and drag her back home by the hair . . ."

"But it would all end in his wife having nervous tension," said Uncle Giorgio, in the voice of an eager pupil. "When she came to, that is," he added.

"Well, anyway," said Aquila, for the first time looking at Uncle Giorgio narrowly (but Giorgio's face was altogether serious). "Well anyway, it is no answer to the problem."

"No," agreed Uncle Giorgio. "Unless, of course, he hits her over the head with his club again."

"That is no answer to any problem," Aquila objected.

"I suppose not. Just rough-and-ready, end-or-mend. Still, it prevented the cave-*man* from having nervous tension, at least," said Uncle Giorgio. "Or don't you think so?"

"Are you suggesting that I hit Anisetta over the head with a club?"

"Oh, dear me, no," protested Giorgio, "not with a *club.*"

Aquila sighed.

"But you know," he said, "there's enough of the irrational beast in me to wish that I could."

Uncle Giorgio's eyes lit up. For a man with a plan, the most dangerous moment is when victory is first glimpsed. That is when most men grow careless. But not Uncle Giorgio.

"Yet after all," he said, "as you were saying at lunchtime, Anisetta is a free agent, at least according to modern notions. She has a mind of her own."

"Mind," echoed Aquila bitterly. "Do you call that a mind?"

"And as you argued during tea, when all is said and done, men are unfaithful to their wives. Why shouldn't women claim the right to be unfaithful to their husbands? In this second half of the twentieth century, as you remarked, surely we have at least learned to treat the sexes as equal."

"Equal!" said Aquila. "Equal! I should just like to know where the equality comes in. Have I ever been unfaithful to Anisetta? Did I ever go to festas with other girls? Have I ever in thought, word or deed been unfaithful to her since I fell in love with her when I was eleven-and-a-half? Equality! You can't have equality unless you start level."

"Well, maybe Anisetta has jumped the gun," Giorgio admitted. "But then again, I am sure Professor Lissom is an accomplished lover. I am certain he knows how to entwine himself round a woman's heart. Little attentions, little courtesies, you know the sort of thing."

A black look crossed Aquila's face, and his eyes, always the index of a rise in the Sicilian's quick temper, grew narrow.

"Cream cakes," said Aquila. "Fool that I am. Cream cakes. She as good as told me so."

"But then what are you to do?" asked Uncle Giorgio.

"Do?" asked Aquila absently, his face working.

"Yes. How can a progressive young man like yourself be expected to meet the situation? Do people expect you to dash up to Professor Lissom saying, 'Give me back my wife!' and then smack his face?"

"Or kick him in the teeth," said Aquila sombrely.

"You can't be expected to act like some character out of the eighteenth century and knock your rival down."

"And jump on him," muttered Aquila.

"Why," said Uncle Giorgio, "before we know where we are we shall be back to horsewhips."

"Too long: too clumsy: get tangled," said Aquila, brooding.

"And," pursued Giorgio, "we'll all be no better than Sicilians, and when a man steals away our wives with soft words and lying promises . . ."

"Poor innocent little Anisetta," said Aquila under his breath, "straight from her native village into the clutches of that villain."

". . . we'll be going out with a gun to shoot him."

"Shooting's too good for him," said Aquila loudly, banging the table. "He should be thrown to wild dogs."

"Or flung off a cliff."

"Or hung over a slow fire upside down," roared Aquila, jumping to his feet.

"Instead of sitting in a cosy little cottage making love to

another man's wife and laughing," said Uncle Giorgio, "laughing in our faces."

"Well, why the blazes are you sitting there talking your head off?" shouted Aquila, his Sicilian blood at last on the boil. "Have you no family pride? Does the name Morales mean nothing to you? Will you let this man Lissom spit upon us? Why are we hiding away here? Why aren't we at the villain's throat? Where is he?" stormed Aquila, while the hotel porter and the manageress stood, open-mouthed, in the doorway whither they had run to see what was causing the disturbance. *"Where is he?"*

"Lilac Cottage, Dribble, near Birmingham," said Uncle Giorgio, springing to his feet.

"Well, how do we get there?" Aquila bellowed.

"Train," said Uncle Giorgio waving two tickets which he produced from his waistcoat pocket. "I've had them since this morning. I thought you'd *never* get moving," he said. And then, making for the door:

"The bags!" he cried to the hotel porter.

"The bill!" he cried to the manageress, while Aquila, his eyes blazing cried, in Sicilian:

"Vengeance!"

CHAPTER V

THE THREE DULL WIVES OF LISSOM

At Oxford station Lissom handed Anisetta into a train. The guard blew his whistle, the train moved off, and Anisetta had to all intents begun to live in sin.

Her first words as a wicked woman were these:

"*Ebbene, siamo q'a.*"

These three words are greatly used by Sicilians. Together they make up the simple statement:

'Well, here we are.'

St. Thomas Aquinas, having remarked upon the same thing, built a gigantic philosophy upon it. Although St. Thomas was called the Dumb Ox of Sicily, his is not the right reply.

The right reply was made by Lissom and in good Sicilian, a language he had learned to speak on several holidays on the island. He said:

"*Ebbene, siamo q'a.*"

The ice should have been broken by this. But Anisetta appeared uncertain and ill at ease.

After a moment she said thoughtfully:

"I hope everything will be all right."

"Are you worrying about how your young husband will take it?" asked Professor Lissom.

"Yes," said Anisetta.

Professor Lissom took her hand in his.

"I shouldn't worry at all," he said. "Your husband will behave like a civilized man."

Anisetta nodded sadly.

"Yes," she said, "I'm afraid he will."

"Does your husband know my country address?" asked Lissom.

"Oh, no," said Anisetta. "You told me not to tell him and I didn't."

"Then everything's *quite* all right," said Lissom, taking her other hand.

Anisetta thought a moment.

"Yes," she said at last. For after all, even if Aquila was civilized there was always Uncle Giorgio. And she had told him. 'Lilac Cottage, Dribble, near Birmingham' she had written, and, last thing before she left the hotel, slipped it under her uncle's bedroom door.

Lilac Cottage, as Anisetta soon discovered, was not really near Dribble. It was not near anything at all. The cottage was surrounded by a garden, the garden was surrounded by trees, the trees were surrounded by a tall hedge, and the hedge was surrounded by a remarkably lonely stretch of English countryside. Professor Lissom's retreat was as carefully hidden as Crusoe's cave: the resemblance went even further. On the door at which Professor Lissom now rang was a plate which said 'Robinson.'

The door was opened by a grey-haired woman dressed in a uniform so starched that every time she moved it made a noise like pasteboard armor. She smiled very happily upon them both and stood aside to let them in. But Lissom first with great courtesy made an introduction.

"Mrs. Morales," he said, "this is Miss Clementine Tripp, my faithful housekeeper for many years. Miss Tripp," he said, changing to English, "This is Mrs. Morales from Sicily. She does not speak very much English but I'm sure you'll know how to make her comfortable for all that. Did you get my telegram?"

"Yes, sir," said Miss Tripp, smiling again at Anisetta.

"Then breakfast, if I know my invaluable Miss Tripp, will be piping hot on the stove."

"It probably is at that, sir," she said and then to Anisetta: "Come along in, my dear, you must be tired having to get up so early." She laid a motherly hand on Anisetta's shoulder and led her into the cottage.

They went into a room furnished so splendidly that Anisetta lowered both her eyes and her voice thinking she was in the side-chapel of a church. There was a painting of the Virgin and Child in a gold frame, a profusion of elaborate gold and silver candle-sticks such as are used on altars, and running down the middle of an oak table a piece of embroidery of great beauty that Anisetta instantly saw was made of pieces of the chasubles prescribed for use on days devoted to Martyrs.

Lissom, noticing her awed look, threw himself into a chair and said:

"I'm glad you like my furnishings, my dear. They're all odds and ends I picked up in junk shops when I was last in your part of the world. The Madonna isn't bad. I like it. But it's only worth the price of its frame, or so I'm told by experts. We'll have breakfast in here, Clementine," he finished, as his housekeeper went about her business.

Anisetta was shocked. She was unused to the Protestant's habit of making their churches look like living rooms, and their living rooms look like churches. But with Miss Tripp's excellent breakfast inside her, Anisetta felt less as though she were attending Mass; and when, puffing at his pipe, Lissom showed her over the six handsomely appointed rooms of Lilac Cottage, she had to admit that it was all most beautiful.

She admired particularly Professor Lissom's book-lined study, so silent with its thick carpet and heavy window hangings. It was here that he had retired to write his sensational monograph on the education of children, the book that was chiefly responsible for the rise of progressive schools. Some people had even called it the Children's Magna Carta, because Professor Lissom had proved beyond doubt of anybody but sadists and reactionaries that children should be allowed to be as free as the summer wind, and to show it by making as much noise as they pleased. Anisetta admired the garden with its border of trees and hedge that gave it utter seclusion. No casual passer-by could get so much as a glimpse of the cottage windows. It was in this garden that Professor Lissom, in the congenial company of one of his most dazzling female admirers, planned and in part wrote that classic counterblast to Victorian secrecy about sex, 'Apropos of Lady Chatterly.'

At eleven they had sherry. Sunk in a more comfortable chair than any she had ever sat in, drinking alcohol at what in Sicily would have been thought an abandoned hour, it would not be true to say that Anisetta felt at home. But she did feel, for the first time, that there might be places not far inferior to Monte Tauro. She even began to like her lover.

But at that very moment Lissom said:

"I do apologize, my dear, but I have to run into Birmingham to see the Midland radio people. I am doing a broadcast tomorrow. I shall be back," he said, with that frank look that he made popular among England's under twenty-fives, "tonight!" Then he told her about how famous he was for answering questions.

Anisetta, a little relieved (and a little hurt) at being left alone, twiddled her glass of sherry for a moment and then asked:

"Supposing somebody wrote to you and said, 'I want to run away with another man's wife. Would this be all right, Professor?' What would you answer?"

Professor Lissom bent his widest smile upon her.

"I should say, 'My dear fellow, it all depends on how fast you can run.' "

With that he kissed her good-bye for the present and went.

Anisetta, finishing off her sherry, looked at the picture of the Madonna and wondered what was keeping Uncle Giorgio and her husband.

Then, very sensibly deciding that wondering would do no good, and being tired from her early rising, she went to sleep.

*   *   *

She awoke suddenly to hear a voice calling her name. She sat upright, rubbed her eyes and looked eagerly about her, hoping to see Aquila or at the very least Uncle Giorgio.

Instead she saw standing over her and gazing into her face with inscrutable expressions, three tall women.

One of the women had a veil draped around her head as though she were dead and in her shroud.

Another of the women had a female head on a man's body.

The third, most frightening of all, was dressed like a soldier: but she had the face of a china doll.

Anisetta said rapidly:

"Santa Maria San Giuseppe San Antonio San Francesco Santa Teresa Sant'Agata San Pancrazio San Michele Archangelo pray for me."

At that she stopped. She could not remember the name of one single saint more than the meagre list that she had just gone through. It was very terrible: in Monte Tauro she knew the whole Litany and as everybody knew, nothing less than the whole Litany was ever really effective in a crisis. But her mind had gone blank. She decided that it was the first fruits of living in sin.

The doll so horribly dressed as a soldier bent forward. She spoke in Italian but with a strange and fearsome accent.

"I . . . am . . . Mrs. Lissom," she said.

She waved her woman's hand with its military cuff towards the figure in the shroud.

"And this . . . is . . . Mrs. Lissom," she said.

She waved her hand towards the man with a woman's head.

"And *this* is Mrs. Lissom."

She looked at Anisetta closely. Anisetta stared back at her, wide-eyed.

"Three Mrs. Lissoms," said the doll. "The third," she said, pointing to herself. "The second," pointing to the shrouded one, "and the first." At which she pointed to the epicene. Then she said, unexpectedly:

"It's the first of the month."

By this time Anisetta was sure that she was in Hell and had all eternity before her. This therefore seemed a pettifogging remark. She did not change her frightened stare.

"My," said the woman in uniform, "you look as though you had seen a ghost."

This second remark, though less trivial than the other, seemed to Anisetta to be nevertheless verging on triteness. Regrettable as it was, the damned could scarcely expect to see anything but ghosts.

However, the woman had spoken not too unkindly. And there was no smell of smoke. Possibly—just possibly—this was not Hell but Purgatory. Cautiously Anisetta began to look about her. For a moment she saw nothing familiar. Then she saw the church candlesticks. Next, with great relief, the picture of the Madonna.

At the very moment that she realized she was still alive, the woman who spoke strange Italian said:

"Of course there's no Mrs. Lissom really just at present because we've all been divorced. But we always try to have a little get-together on the first of every month and we were wondering if you would care to join us."

"Please do," said the epicene, and smiled.

She was Clementine Tripp. She had changed her uniform for a masculine tweed jacket and slacks. But she was certainly Miss Tripp.

"But . . .," said Anisetta, and her mouth fell open.

"Now don't you worry about anything," said the woman in uniform. "We shall explain everything after lunch. I know it must be very confusing for you. It's even confusing for Professor Lissom sometimes. But it's a habit that's grown on us and I'm sure there's no harm in it. Now, how about a tiny little cocktail?" she asked.

Anisetta nodded vigorously. She had never had a cocktail before, but she hoped after this shock, that it would not be too tiny.

It was big enough to give her courage to ask, when she had drunk it:

"If you are all Mrs. Lissoms, why is one Mrs. Lissom dressed like a man, another Mrs. Lissom dressed like a corpse, and why are you dressed like a soldier?"

"That," said the woman in uniform, "we shall tell you after we have had lunch."

*   *   *

When lunch was over all the women lit cigarettes and the one in uniform began:

"You must first know that I am not dressed as a soldier: I am dressed as an air-hostess. The second Mrs. Lissom is not dressed as a corpse: she is dressed as the principal wife of an Eastern potentate: and the last Mrs. Lissom (although I should really call her the first) is not dressed as a man but wears the sensible outfit that is considered appropriate for housekeepers by the Directress of the School of Sound Home Management, of which she is an alumna. How she came to be an alumna, how the other came to be in a harem and how I came to be in an aeroplane (and so learned to speak Italian, which you will find convenient as our stories proceed) we shall now begin to tell you."

With that the housekeeper lit another cigarette from the butt of her first, and said—the air-hostess translating:

"As you may know, my dear, Professor Lissom, our husband, is a genius."

"Yes," said the other two women, "our husband is a genius."

"So, of course," went on the housekeeper, "he is very unhappy."

"Yes," agreed the other two women, "so of course he is unhappy."

When Anisetta had heard this preface in Italian, she said:

"But if *I* were a genius I would not be unhappy: I would be delighted. Besides, my Uncle Giorgio is a genius. He is the greatest brigand since Mussolino—"

At which the air-hostess interrupted her and said:

"I do not think we should discuss politics. Besides, our husband was a great admirer of his. He was the first to point out that he made the trains run on time."

"I said Mussolin*o*," said Anisetta. "He was a famous Calabrian brigand. In Italian you have to be very careful of your endings. Anyway, what I wanted to say was that Uncle Giorgio is a genius and he is not at all unhappy."

"Well," said the housekeeper, "he is an Italian and that may be different. But every Englishman knows that all English geniuses are unhappy. Byron was unhappy because he loved his sister. Dr. Johnson was unhappy because he was afraid of Hell: and Shakespeare might have been happy as Shakespeare, but as a matter of fact he was very unhappy indeed because he was Bacon."

Anisetta did not altogether follow this but she merely said: "Oh," because the alumna of the School of Sound Home Management did not look like a woman who would brook much contradiction.

"It is quite obvious that it must be so," said the housekeeper. "We cannot all be geniuses, but we are a democratic nation. So geniuses must be unhappy to balance things up. Now if you will promise not to interrupt, I shall go on with my story."

The air-hostess did not translate this, but simply looked at Anisetta and laid a finger to her lips.

"When I first met Bustle," went on the housekeeper, "he was very unhappy indeed because he could never make up his mind whether to have steak-and-kidney pudding with chips and coffee to follow, or steak-and-kidney pudding without chips, and apple dumpling to follow. He could not afford to have both chips and dumpling, and he was very partial to both. In fact, he was very partial to anything in the shape of food because he was living on what they call a University Exhibition, though what either the University or the scholars have got to show off about with such a miserly sum of money, I never could see. But I did see that Frankie Lissom was a genius."

"How?" asked Anisetta, before anyone could stop her.

"Because I was in love with him," said the housekeeper, "and since nobody could say he was either good-looking or rich, he had to be a genius. You're a woman yourself: what would you have thought?"

Anisetta had this translated twice. In the end she said:
"I would have thought exactly the same thing."

"Well then," said the housekeeper, "I saw to it that Frankie
got steak-and-kidney pudding, apple dumpling *and* cream *and*
coffee to follow, all for the same amount of money. It was quite
easy because at that time I was a waitress in the "Presto" cafe
next to the British Museum Library where Frankie used to
come for his one meal a day. I used to make up the difference
out of my own money sometimes, but usually I overcharged
any woman that I saw Frankie making eyes at while he was
having lunch. The only time a woman isn't sharp on her money
is when she thinks she's being admired by a man, and *then*
she's an absolute fool. That is why the vacuum cleaner is such
a great commercial success."

She lit another cigarette from the stub of her last while the
air-hostess put this into Italian, the air-hostess adding, "Remember, do not interrupt." But Anisetta, awed by so much
perspicacity about the ways of her sex, had no intention of
doing so.

"A little while after that," went on the housekeeper, "he
asked me to his lodgings. He had one room in Mecklenburg
Square and you've never seen such a pigsty in your life. It
wasn't Bohemian. In those days it used to cost at least four
pounds a week in unearned income to be Bohemian. You
couldn't live a carefree life in a great gaunt studio largely
furnished with empty bottles unless you could first rent a studio.
That cost two quid. Then there was the bottles. Frankie had a
bed-sitting room. He had plenty of bottles, it's true, but they
mostly contained stomach medicines. Although I could guarantee him his steak-and-kidney pudding, I couldn't guarantee
what was in it. As for the room, Frankie had done his best with
it. He had covered in the wash basin with a sort of box, in the
hope that it would look like a small sideboard: but it just
looked like a commode. He had covered the bed with a rug
and some cushions in the hope that it would make the room
look like a lounge, but it only made it look like a room in a
rather nice brothel. The one good thing about the room as

Frankie rented it was that it had a decent light hanging plumb in the center, with a sensible glass shade that left the bulb bare. Frankie had draped extension cords all round the place so that he could have little lamps with parchment shades. When he switched them on all you could see of him without your eyes watering was his shoes: and they didn't add anything to the air of solid comfort for which Frankie's young soul yearned. And everything in the room was hanging with dirt."

She drew heavily on her cigarette, and then dabbed her eyes, with much by-play to make clear that it was due to the smoke.

"Poor Frankie," she said and laughed. She fell silent for a minute, looking at the table-cloth. Then she went on:

"He talked to me about politics and socialism and how there was going to be a revolution to sweep away the decaying fabric of capitalist civilization. I've never forgotten his words. Who could? There was enough decaying fabric hanging round that bed-sitter to run a paper-mill."

And when the air-hostess boggled in making this clear Anisetta said: "Never mind. Let her go on. She's going to marry him in a minute. I know she is. She talked about his boots. When I fell in love with Aquila his boots went straight to my heart. He never cleaned them behind, and it always looked so pathetic when he turned his back."

"Frankie asked me," said the housekeeper, "what I thought about his views on the structure of society. I told him that I thought he needed the loving care of a capable woman. Then the landlady brought in the tea. Being in a tea-shop, I knew a few of the tricks. I looked in the pot: as I expected it was full of old tea-leaves topped off with a little new. The butter was half-margarine: there was water in the milk. Without a word I took the tray straight downstairs to the basement where the landlady lived. I told her what I thought of her. She told me what she thought of me. She called me Frankie's trollop. Then I sniffed significantly and asked her about her drains. Drains are a landlady's nightmare. They cost a fortune to repair. I also mentioned that I was not a trollop. I was

Frankie's young lady and we were going to be married at Easter. After that she made a real tea, I took it up to Frankie, Frankie ate it and we were married at Easter."

"You were very happy," said the woman whose head was wrapped up like a corpse. "Frankie often talked about it."

"We were," said the housekeeper, lighting yet another cigarette. "Frankie never looked back, from that first decent tea I got for him, down to this very minute. He got a job in London University and I left my tea-shop. Very soon we could afford to rent a real tumble-down studio and live as though we hadn't a penny in the world. Everybody knew we were really quite comfortably off, so it was very enjoyable. Frankie was still very interested in the overthrow of society but he didn't talk so much about it. Meantime I did what I'd always wanted to do from the time I saw Frankie looking at a menu: I made him a comfortable home."

She looked round the dining room for a moment before going on, the polish on the furniture bringing an answering gleam to her eye.

"Then one day Frankie said to me, 'You know, I sometimes think I take too gloomy a view of life. Things are in a very bad way with the world, of course; they couldn't be worse. But after all, one must have faith in human nature. Human nature is wonderful, human nature is full of surprises. We must not set a limit in our minds as to what human nature is capable of doing.' So of course," said the housekeeper with a touch of sadness, "I knew he had a mistress."

"Me," said the woman with the cloth wrapped round her head. Anisetta observing the woman who said this more closely, now saw that she had ruby studs as ear-rings, and a somewhat freckled complexion under her make-up.

The housekeeper nodded.

"Yes, you."

She turned back to Anisetta. "They met at a party in our studio. It was a sort of reception to all the delegates to a Sexological Conference. You are too young to understand what a

Sexological Conference means. Come to that, I think many of the delegates were too. But they were very fashionable among intelligent people just then. The idea behind them was to get the laws altered so that everybody could make love in just the fashion he or she wanted. People would get up one after the other and defend the most shocking vices. My cheeks burned to hear the mere names of the vices, that is, when I found out what the names meant. They were usually in Latin. For such free and easy people there was a surprising lot of Latin going around. I remember they all kept using a word that a certain Mr. Havelock Ellis was fond of: *nates,* it was. I thought it must mean something awful. When I looked it up in the dictionary and found that it was Latin for 'backside' I was really quite surprised. I think these delegates must have been ever so nicely brought up to be too shy to use a word like that in their own mother tongue. But I had quite a lot of surprises in one way and another. At the beginning I used to mark down some man or other who was calling for freedom to do such-and-such, and say to myself, 'That man will never set foot in my house.' But it always turned out that he was respectably married with two bouncing babies, and he was just defending such-and-such out of kindness of heart for others. In fact most of the sexologists were as pure as the newly fallen snow, though unfortunately not so silent. For all that, sex was in the air, and very much so."

She gave a long look at the woman who had said she was Lissom's mistress.

"Frankie used to write article after article about it. He was particularly keen that women should have full freedom to realize their passionate nature. He used to say, 'Clementine, are you in love with anyone?' 'Only you, Frankie,' I used to say. 'Yes,' he used to answer, quite cross, 'but I'm your husband.' 'Well,' I would answer, 'I've only time for one husband.' Then he would say, 'Clementine, you say that in just the way you used to tell customers in the tea-shop that you'd only got one pair of hands.' Then he would snatch his hat and go out to spend the night with . . ."

60   THE BACKWARD BRIDE

"Me," said the woman in the shroud and earrings.

"I did my best," said the housekeeper. "I could see his point. After all the trouble he and his friends had gone to, winning our sexual freedom, what was I doing with it? Nothing. I had about as much use for sexual freedom as a tambourine girl in the Salvation Army. Housekeeping was my pleasure. But not wanting to let down the twentieth century, I tried to combine the two. I had a flirtation with the milkman. Frankie was quite pleased, and it would have all gone quite well if only I'd stuck to milk. But like a fool I had to ask my lover if he couldn't manage to bring round some nice eggs each day. He did and they were scandalous, at least, for the price he asked. I could get better and cheaper at the Co-op round the corner. I told him so and he didn't disagree. I could never look upon him quite the same again. I tried to transfer my affections to the man who collected the rent each week. But Frankie did so well he paid by cheque. Then there was nothing for it but to agree to a divorce. Frankie said we were incompatible; he said I had as much passion as a rolling-pin. He said he wanted his freedom to marry someone else."

"Me," said the woman in the shroud. "And he did. I had five lovers and I was sitting on the Bastardy Committee which was trying to move Parliament to pass new laws about illegitimacy. I was very advanced indeed and at first Frankie and I were divinely happy."

"They certainly were," agreed the housekeeper.

"Except for my cooking," said the other woman.

"And your taste in furnishing."

"And my sewing," the second Mrs. Lissom cheerfully agreed.

"So being a free woman with a right to my own mind, I insisted on being their housekeeper," said Clementine. "I didn't put it like that. I said that I hoped they would not stand in the way of my self-fulfilment. What I wanted to do was to look after Frankie and see that he got plenty to eat. I always did. I always shall. So with Frankie's alimony I took courses at the School of Sound Home Management and I passed with distinction. I've been with Professor Lissom ever since to our mutual satisfaction."

"I wish I could say the same," said the second Mrs. Lissom. "And I'm sure it wasn't Frankie's fault. Frankie fell in love with me because I was in love with five other men. I was his ideal of an intelligent woman who not only knew her own mind, but knew her own body. A man called D. H. Lawrence insisted that it was very, very important. But then he was a man. And I often think a man's body behaves much more conventionally than a woman's. Because, you see, the moment I married Frankie I stopped wanting any of my five other lovers. I was annoyed with myself, and I think Frankie was pretty disappointed, too. I read Shelley and Keats and lots of wicked French novels and tried to think that passion was the greatest thing in a woman's life. But it wasn't: not in mine. The greatest thing in my life was getting letters addressed to *Mrs. Lissom*. And it wasn't the *Lissom* part that gave me the thrill. It was the *Mrs.* You see, my dear, the reason that I had so many lovers before I was married was not that I wanted a lot; I was just dead scared I wouldn't have any. I wasn't in the grip of passion; I was taking out insurance policies against being an old maid. I wasn't flinging myself into the pleasures of life; I was keeping myself out of the Governesses' Benevolent Institution in my old age. I wasn't a splendid whore; I was a husband-hunter."

"It's funny how few really splendid whores there've been," said the housekeeper. "You can't wonder at them being snapped up by kings when they do turn up. Madame du Barry and Pompadour deserved their success, I always say. It's not many women who can do what they did; just as there's not many woman who can conduct an orchestra. We women are a limited lot."

She shook her head sadly and lit another cigarette.

The second Mrs. Lissom looked at her for a moment as she puffed out the smoke in an efficient and manly manner.

"Yes," she said admiringly, "but at least you were fond of Frankie when you'd got him. And you still are."

"Very fond," agreed the housekeeper. "Except when he buys knick-knacks that pick up the dust," and she glanced disapprovingly at the ornate candlesticks.

"It was the beginning of a career for you," went on the second Mrs. Lissom, "but for me it was the end. I'd not been married six months when Frankie said to me, 'Deirdre, you give me the impression that, no doubt in spite of yourself, your passion has cooled towards me.' I said, 'Do I, Frankie? I'm awfully sorry. I must pull myself up.' 'I don't want you to pull yourself up,' said Frankie, very irritably, 'I want you to let yourself go!' Well, I did my best."

"You did," agreed the housekeeper. "I got quite worried about you. You wouldn't eat a thing I put in front of you. You were trying so hard it quite took your appetite away."

The second Mrs. Lissom nodded. "But I think I'm just a naturally dull woman," she said, "because the only thing I could think of doing was to have a baby. That was the end. The baby was sweet, of course, but now I was not only a Mrs., I was a mother. As for poor Frankie, well, as he said himself, he wasn't my lover any more, he was just a vital statistic. So we divorced."

"Much against my advice, I must say," said the housekeeper. "A tidier woman than you I never did see. But I was busy with my housekeeping exams at the time and the thing was done while I was swotting up Hygiene."

The air-hostess interrupted the story at this point to tell Anisetta that the housekeeper was the leading authority on home hygiene in England. She even gave talks on the radio.

The housekeeper blushed slightly and said, "Yes, but we don't mention it here. One of the rules the School insisted upon was that a housekeeper must never give the impression of having interests outside the four walls of her place of employment."

"*I* had to look for a career too," said the second Mrs. Lissom, recapturing the conversation. "And I fell on my feet. I found something to which I was exactly fitted by temperament and experience."

"You did," agreed the housekeeper, and she ran an approving eye over the drapery around the second Mrs. Lissom's head.

"What was that?" asked Anisetta eagerly.

"I met a distinguished gentleman from a Far Eastern country," she said. "He already had three wives, whom he described as being without doubt the most beautiful women in the Fertile Crescent—he was a Ph.D. in history. He was passionately in love with one of them but he said she had not the brains to cope with the duties of a principal wife. Principal wives' duties, he explained, had greatly expanded with the spread of Westernization—he was a Ph.D. of Balliol, by the way—and since he had his eye on a political career he wanted someone who could entertain graciously. He was kind enough to say that I was the very woman he had been looking for. He proposed marriage; quite formally, down on one knee and in a conservatory. Of course I jumped at it. If I was the woman he wanted, he was certainly the man *I'd* been looking for. I could be a wife in public and not be a bit bothered in private. The three most beautiful women in the Fertile Crescent would look after that. And to give them due credit, I must say they always have. I've met them once or twice: charming girls, I found them, though a bit giggly. I don't see much of them. My husband does most of his political entertaining here in England and he prefers me to remain most of my time in London."

"He's considered a rising man, so I'm told," said the air-hostess.

"He's doing very well," said the second Mrs. Lissom with a stately bow. "Just now he's delegate to the United Nations Committee drawing up the international convention for the Rights of Women. I can't say his heart is in his work, but he obeys his Government's instructions and makes very progressive speeches. They chose him from very sensible motives. They said that he should know more about women than most people, with four wives, and all happy. It was quite a little tribute to our harem, we felt. And so, my dear, you now know why I wear this thing over my head. I wear it to please my husband, because it is a national dress, but also because I am fond of it. It symbolizes for me the happiest years of my life and I hope it will show other women wherever I go the way to be married without irksome responsibilities."

"And I wear this sensible tailor-made when I'm off-duty," said the housekeeper, indicating her suit, "in the hope that some married women who are trying to please their romantic husbands will realize that God made some women feminine and some women distinctly not."

"As for me," said the air-hostess, "to tell you the truth, I'm wearing my uniform because I'm due on duty in half an hour, so I'll make my story short. When Lissom met me I had even more lovers than *she* did," and she smiled at the second Mrs. Lissom, who smiled back.

"Lissom thought I went to bed with all of them, but then I've always found that in matters of elementary sex-knowledge, men are like schoolboys and they'll believe the most impossible things. Frankie thought that I had flung myself into the pleasures of the senses, but all I wanted was a bit of company. Clementine here says that it's a funny thing that there aren't any women conductors of orchestras. Well, for that matter, has anybody ever heard of a woman hermit? It's unthinkable. A woman has got to have somebody to gossip with or she'd burst. Look at all those women who were saints. What did most of them do the moment they got their own way? Set up a brand new convent and surrounded themselves with a whole lot of clacking nuns. But most women don't count other women as company; they interrupt too much. No, what a woman wants is a man who'll listen and say 'Yes, dear,' and 'No, dear,' at the right times and once in a while start a new topic of conversation. *Start*," she emphasized. "You can't really have a good gossip with a boy friend either; if they're in love with you they're fidgety all the time. When Frankie proposed to me he was nice and middle-aged and just the man I was looking for. I did my best for him. I tried to produce an atmosphere of abandonment to the pleasures of sex. But after we'd been married six months, Frankie said there was just about as much abandonment in our home as there was in the smoking-room of his club. Well, when all's said and done, a good chat in friendly surroundings is what most women crave for, and I was not really to blame. So our marriage broke up; but I can't say I've ever been sorry. I got a job almost straight away as an air-hostess and I've had the time of my life. I can talk to my heart's content—it's part of my job to get friendly with passengers—and the housework's cut down to serving box-luncheons. Some of the passengers get fresh with me, of course, and sex rears its ugly head. But I always say, 'Now Mr. Robinson, you'll forget all about it when we touch down,' and what's more they do. No," she said, glancing at her wristwatch and giving a pat to her cap, "to be in the arms of her mate is woman's greatest pleasure no doubt, but only provided she lacks outside interests."

"So you see," said the first Mrs. Lissom, "we've all three failed Frankie."

"And Frankie is very unhappy," said the second Mrs. Lissom.

"And that's why we're looking to you," said the third Mrs. Lissom.

"We're hoping," said the housekeeper, "that for once Frankie has found a woman who will live up to his ideal."

"Because we women," said the second Mrs. Lissom, "are a dull lot, generally speaking."

"And when you think of all the trouble Frankie has gone to getting us our sexual freedom, well, you can't help feeling you owe him something."

"You mean," said Anisetta, "you're hoping I'm a . . . a splendid whore?"

"My dear," said the second Mrs. Lissom, taking her hand, "He's such a genius. And we women know it's such a *little* thing."

With that, the second Mrs. Lissom left for a Unesco tea party, the first Mrs. Lissom went to her pantry, and the third Mrs. Lissom got into a small motor-car, saying to Anisetta:

"See you again on the first of next month."

And with that she drove off to her airport.

CHAPTER VI

ANISETTA FLY-BY-NIGHT

Late that night Francis Lissom said to Anisetta:
"Happy?"
Anisetta, who wanted to stop him talking in case she should miss the sound of a car (carrying, she hoped, her frantic husband) said:
"Ooo yes."
Still later that night Francis Lissom said to Anisetta:
"Happy?"
And Anisetta in a black rage with her husband for not yet appearing said:
"Yes, of course. Why do you keep asking?"
"Well," said Lissom, nettled, "nobody has ever objected to being asked before."
"It sounds so silly," said Anisetta, thumping the cushions of the divan to make it more comfortable.
"Well, what would you have me say?" asked Lissom. "How do you like:

> Negli occhi porta la mia donna Amore;
> Per che si fa gentil ciò ch' ella mira:
> Ov' ella passa, ogni uom vêr lei si gira,
> E cui saluta fa tremar lo core."

"Certainly not," said Anisetta, "that makes me sound like a trollop," and then remorse struck her because she remembered that Frankie was a genius and a trollop is just what she ought to be.
"All the same," she said to gain herself (and Aquila) time, "it sounds quite nice. Say it again."
Lissom did. He said—and handsomely too:

66

"My lady carries love within her eyes;
All that she looks on is made pleasanter;
Upon her path men turn to gaze at her;
He whom she greeteth feels his heart to rise."

But there was still no Aquila.

Sicilians are not a very patient people: and Anisetta was not the most patient of Sicilians. Anisetta counted ten, slowly; heard no car, and made up her mind.

She leaned back among the cushions, put her arms above her head, and said:

"Ah! How wonderful it is to be free: how wonderful to follow one's natural instincts. How lovely, Frankie, to be able to do just what I want."

She put her arm around Lissom's neck, and kissed him full upon the lips.

*　　*　　*

"Faster! Faster!" cried Aquila. He leaned far forward, narrowing his eyes against the rush of wind.

An elderly lady poked him gently with her umbrella.

"It is dangerous to lean out of the window, young man," she said in a kindly voice.

Aquila looked round.

"Cosa?" he said.

"É pericoloso to lean out of il finestra," said the elderly lady who had but recently been to Florence.

Aquila obediently withdrew his head and sat down.

"I'm afraid this is a very slow train," said the elderly lady. "We are already running half an hour late. Nationalization does not seem to have done much to improve the railways, I must say."

Aquila's eyes lit up.

"Really?" he said. "Is that your considered opinion? How interesting. Of course the whole problem of state ownership is one of the most crucial that faces the democratic state."

"It is so refreshing to get a foreigner's view on our social experiment," said the elderly lady. "Now tell me, what are your first impressions?"

Aquila told her. In the opposite corner Uncle Giorgio looked at his watch, sighed, and fell into a gentle doze.

*   *   *

Anisetta heard Lissom mutter, as he passionately kissed her hand:

"Tell me anything—*anything*—that you want and I will give it to you."

Simultaneously she heard the noise of a motor-car engine in the distance.

Her instinct told her that it was her husband. Her mountain upbringing told her what to do.

"Frankie," she said, "I do want to be a splendid whore, really I do, but just now what I want most of anything in the world is a plate of *spaghetti al pomodoro,* because I am suddenly very hungry."

*   *   *

Lissom abruptly stopped kissing her hand. This was what Anisetta had expected. She had relied on her belief that no gentleman would seduce a hungry woman. This may not be wholly true. Some gentlemen, if very young gentlemen, might try. But neither they, nor the Devil himself, would have any success.

Lissom, who might be expected to fly into a temper with the whole female sex, was not even angry with Anisetta. He was merely annoyed at himself for not having asked Miss Tripp to stock a tin of Anisetta's favorite food.

This forbearance is not to his credit. It is a mechanism of Nature, as marvellous as a peacock's tail, to make sure that the race will continue. Without it, Trappist monasteries, an obvious and logical place for all men after a brief sowing of wild oats, would dot every mountainside in the world. With it, they

are few and far between. It was this marvellous mechanism
which made Lissom say with great mildness:

"Unless you would like some chocolates which I always
keep handy, I am afraid that I will have to get out the car and
take you into Birmingham. There is a little Italian restaurant
there which might still be open."

Anisetta said:

"Well come on, let's *go*."

*   *   *

"Thank you for a very fair-minded explanation of the case
for and against state ownership," said Aquila to the elderly
lady, after listening to her with complete absorption for fifteen
minutes. "I cannot help admiring your British impartiality. As
a guest on your shores may I say that nowhere but in England
can one hear politics discussed without heat and without par-
tisan feeling. Indeed, I could go on listening to you for the next
hour but I am afraid that I must wake my Uncle Giorgio,
because this, regrettably, is where we get off."

With that he tugged Giorgio's sleeve. When Giorgio was
awake, they both got down from the train, Aquila giving the
elderly lady a handsome bow as he stood hat in hand, watching
the train pull out of the station.

"A charming woman," said Aquila to Giorgio, as the tail-
light of the train disappeared round the bend.

"So is your wife," said Giorgio.

"Ah, yes," said Aquila, with a little start of recollection. He
began to stroll towards the station exit.

"Do you know," said Aquila, as Giorgio gave up the
tickets, "that lady was a lesson to me. What balance! What
reasonableness! How admirably she saw her opponent's point
of view. How superbly British! And look, as a contrast, at me,
rushing after Professor Lissom with my teeth bared like a sav-
age dog, blind to reason, blind to compromise, a hot-headed
Sicilian bent on physical violence. I feel," he said, as Giorgio
hailed a taxi, "that a cooling hand has been laid upon my fore-

head. I'm certain," he said as Giorgio pushed him into the taxi, "that Professor Lissom and I will be able to reason this thing out in perfect friendliness."

"The English," said Aquila with emotion, "are so sane."

*   *   *

"Hurry!" shouted Giorgio through the taxi-window.

The taxi-driver, bulky and middle-aged, turned round with deliberation.

"Hurry?" he said, even more deliberately.

"Yes, hurry," said Uncle Giorgio. "Double fare if you get there in time."

"In time for what?" enquired the taxi-driver as though he were dealing tolerantly with over-eager children.

"Never mind what," said Uncle Giorgio. "Just get there."

"It must be very urgent," said the taxi-driver, but not so tolerantly. In fact, he seemed to be growing stern.

"It is," said Uncle Giorgio.

"So I should think," said the taxi-driver—and now there was no doubt that he was stern—"since you haven't time to remember your manners."

With that he turned back to face his windscreen. He slowly ground the gears of the taxi into their proper position for starting, conveying, by the set of his head, that he would not have cared overmuch if Uncle Giorgio himself were being mauled among the cogs.

Uncle Giorgio squared his jaw.

"Do not get angry, Uncle," said Aquila hastily. "I assure you that bad temper will get you nowhere in England. Besides, it may not be the driver's fault. The taxi may be an old machine."

"I do not know anything about machines, except that I know one way of making them go faster when the driver wants to go slow."

Aquila saw with alarm that a peculiar look had come into his uncle's eye.

"Have you noticed," said Aquila talking very fast and

brightly, "what an intelligent face our driver has? So different from our Sicilian taxi-drivers, who are sometimes of not much higher mentality than the horses they have replaced. It's the wonderful English educational system. Just because a man is doing a menial job, it does not mean, in England, that he is ignorant. On the contrary, I daresay when this man goes home he takes up one of those admirable guides to philosophy, or mathematics or sociology for the million which are such a feature of English life. And I assure you," he said pressingly, as he saw Uncle Giorgio's right hand wander, "that the only way of getting on with the educated democracy of England is to talk to them on their own high intellectual level. Now, for instance, if we want this man to go fast, we should engage him in friendly conversation about some intelligent topic. Can you think of anything?"

"Yes," said Uncle Giorgio, as he produced an automatic pistol: "Ballistics."

Aquila flung himself into the opposite seat, so as to hide Uncle Giorgio from being seen in the driving-mirror.

"Uncle!" he said, "I'm ashamed of you. Is *this* what your wedding present to me has come to? Is *this* the way I'm going to put our violent Sicilian past behind us?"

Uncle Giorgio apologized.

"I'm sorry, Aquila," he said. "I forgot myself."

"You remembered yourself, you mean," said Aquila severely. "Do you realise that nobody in England carries fire-arms except the landed gentry and the criminal classes? If anybody ever sees you with that pistol you must immediately say that you are fond of partridge shooting. Now please put it away. And if we get into any difficulty again promise me you will remember that you are in a civilized country and not resort to firearms, but use your wits."

"I promise," said Uncle Giorgio.

"I think on the whole you'd better give me the gun," said Aquila.

Uncle Giorgio hesitated.

"But of course, if you want to spoil your wedding present

to Anisetta and me, you can keep it," said Aquila. "I'm sure I've had a great deal of fun as it is, and I'm very grateful."

"Oh, please, Aquila," said Uncle Giorgio, greatly distressed. "That is most unkind of you."

Silently Aquila held out his hand. Giorgio laid the gun in it, with a little sigh. Aquila, concealing his movements from the driving-mirror, put the gun in his pocket.

"Now," said Uncle Giorgio to his favorite nephew, "are we friends again?"

"Yes," said Aquila, "but you must let me run things my own way. I know best."

It was because he was firm in this conviction that when they at last drew up beside Lissom's station wagon, and Aquila saw Lissom holding open the door for Anisetta, he acted in the determined manner which I shall now describe.

He leaped from the taxi. Anisetta saw him in the light of the head-lamps.

"Aquila!" she cried. "Oh, *Aquila.*" She ran towards him with outstretched hands.

Aquila seized her. He kissed her on both cheeks and then on the lips.

"I knew you'd come," said Anisetta, when she could get her breath. "I knew it. But what a long time you've been."

"Better late than never," said Aquila lightly.

"*Yes,*" said Anisetta, not at all lightly, thinking of how near she had been to satisfying the claims of unhappy genius. With that thought she looked round to see what had become of Lissom.

Dazzled by the headlights of the taxi, Lissom had not immediately seen what had happened. His vision, however, was now fully restored, and he was legging it up the garden path towards his cottage door as fast as he could go.

"Just a moment, Professor Lissom," Aquila called out in a commanding voice.

Lissom leaped in the air and missing the path plunged for a moment into some rose bushes. He quickly disentangled himself, and continued to make for the safety of the door.

But his accident had given Aquila time to put Anisetta gently aside and start after the Professor with long purposeful strides.

"Ooo!" shrieked Anisetta. "Uncle Giorgio! Where are you? Quick! They're going to fight."

Uncle Giorgio, who was still in the taxi, heard her shout and ran towards her.

"He'll do something terrible," said Anisetta, pointing to the two running figures. "I could see it in his eye."

Giorgio seized her hand and together they ran after the two men. As they reached half-way up the garden path, they saw that Lissom had reached the door.

But it was locked. Desperately Lissom flung himself against it, the dim porch light showing up the agitation of his face. The door stood firm and Lissom with trembling hands began to search for the key.

At that moment Aquila, with a great leap, was beside him on the door-step.

"Professor Lissom," they heard him say. "I may as well be frank. I made this journey with the sole intention of wringing your neck."

"Stop him," shrieked Anisetta to Uncle Giorgio, and then stood squarely in his path so that Giorgio could do nothing of the sort.

They saw Aquila's hand go out.

"But," Aquila went on, "a conversation in the train with one of your countrywomen and an incident in the taxi upon which I will not enlarge has brought me to my senses. I'm sure," he said grasping Lissom's limp hand, "that you and I can talk this matter over like two civilized men whose pride it is to be guided by the light of reason."

Uncle Giorgio made a sudden move to grasp Anisetta.

"Look out!" he shouted to the two men on the door-step.

But he was too late. Anisetta had wrenched herself from his grasp, covered the distance between Giorgio and the door in three strides, and dealt her husband a swinging box on the ears.

Aquila, taken utterly by surprise, reeled off the doorstep, tripped over the foot-wiper that had been placed near it by the tidy Clementine, and sat down heavily on the gravel.

Lissom, seizing this diversion with great promptitude, got out his key, opened the door, and slipped inside the house.

"You," she began. "You, you, *you*," she went on. "Oh, I could . . ." But instead of wasting words on what she could do, she did it.

As Uncle Giorgio came up to the door-step, Anisetta hammered on the door.

"Frankie!" she cried. "Open the door."

Gingerly Frankie opened the door five inches. He saw Aquila on the ground and opened it a little wider. Then he saw Giorgio and not only slammed the door to again but put it on the bolt.

Anisetta instantly pushed open the letter-box.

"*Pronto!*" she said into the letter-box. "*Pronto! Frankie! Pronto!*"

This is a word much used by Italians, and even more by Sicilians. It means 'Ready' but it can be employed with many shades of meaning. Thus, a cook will use it to announce that he is ready to serve dinner, while Anisetta used it now to say that she was ready to sacrifice her virtue.

She defied—no, she invited—Lissom to do his worst. She apologized for having previously hung back. She would do her duty by genius. She would henceforth be a Scarlet Woman.

So she wound up, ". . . take me to Birmingham!"

"I've got an idea worth two of that," said Lissom through the letter-box in a delighted voice.

"Well, open the door and tell it to me," said Anisetta.

"No," said Lissom. "Make a dash for the car. I'll go round by the kitchen garden and meet you in the station wagon. Can you start the engine?"

"Yes," said Anisetta.

"*Darling,*" said Lissom through the door. "I love you."

While all this was going on, Uncle Giorgio was picking up Aquila.

Now neither Giorgio nor Aquila had heard Lissom's plan to go round by the kitchen garden to avoid them. Nor had they heard him advise Anisetta to make a dash for the station wagon. Therefore when they saw her straighten up from speaking through the letter-box, and particularly when she turned towards Aquila with a look of concern, they both thought that she was sorry for what she had done. They were mistaken. Anisetta, like most women, was prepared to admit she might be sorry for what she was going to do, but she would defend to the death anything she had done in the past.

Anisetta said to her husband:

"I do hope the ground was not wet."

"No," said Aquila, with remarkable dignity, considering what had just happened to him, "it was quite dry, but a little hard."

"Good," said Anisetta. "Because wet ground would be so bad for"—and here she paused, balanced on the balls of her feet—"*for your rheumatism,*" she ended, speaking as though she were launching not words but a javelin.

Aquila upon the instant was seized with a speechless and immobilizing rage. Taking the opportunity that she had created for herself (how, I shall explain, but first let her get safely in the car) she leaped from the step, ran down the garden path, clambered into the car and started the engine. Not more than seven seconds later Lissom pelted down the road (having gained it by the back entrance) jumped into the car by the door which Anisetta held open for him and seizing the wheel drove away.

We can all now turn with a certain peace of mind to the question of Aquila's rheumatism.

*　　　*　　　*

It should be clear at the outset that he did not suffer from rheumatism at all. Although he labored under all the mental doubts and conflicts proper to any really up-to-date young man, he was sound in wind and limb. But he had once *said* he had rheumatism, although no doctor would have diagnosed it. He did this for the following reason:

On Monte Tauro's coast-line, very near to the small limestone islands which are called The Cyclades, and not a hundred yards from the promontory which is called 'The Cape of the Sirens,' there is a tall pinnacle of stone jutting from the sea that is called by the Monte Taurans, The Rock. It is about forty feet high. The young men of Monte Tauro take much pride in climbing to the top of this rock, standing like bronze statues silhouetted against the sky until they are sure everybody on the beach is looking at them, and diving from it into the Ionian Sea below. They have a right to be proud. The sea below is not only strewn with rocks; it has a swift current. Unless one is a good diver one will be brained on the rocks; unless one is a good swimmer one will be drowned by the current. Every young man in Monte Tauro is both a good diver and a good swimmer: they all took The Rock in their stride, except our hero.

Up till his eighteenth summer Aquila, like the rest of the boys, had spent nearly all of them splashing about in the water as happily as a spaniel. When he was eighteen he was due to go off The Rock. He climbed to the top; he stood poised like a bronze statue, and then he asked himself, 'Why am I doing this?'

No young man of Monte Tauro had ever asked himself this before. In any case they knew why they were doing it. They wanted to impress the girls on the beach. The only other socially accepted way of impressing them was to be the center-forward in the Monte Tauro football team. But only one man could be center-forward; the rest had to go off The Rock. So off they all went; except Aquila.

Aquila was introspective. 'Am I coward?' he went on. 'Or is there some influence, deep within me, holding me back?' He looked down at the water forty feet below.

'Why am I not like other boys?' he asked himself. He looked once more down at the water. It was inscrutable. He looked at the rocks. They were exceedingly jagged. He climbed down, sunk in self-analysis. He walked thoughtfully to the beach. He saw Anisetta.

Anisetta, hands on her hips, said:

"A fine thing, making me a laughing-stock! What happened?"

Aquila should truthfully have answered, "I suddenly became introspective."

Instead he answered, "I suffer from rheumatism and standing up there in the breeze I felt a twinge."

This is not quite such a lie as it looks. Aquila did not of course suffer from any physical malady whatsoever. But had he mentioned introspection, Anisetta would have thought it a disease in any case.

On the other hand Anisetta knew that Aquila was not telling the exact truth. But partly from pride and partly because she loved him she pretended to believe him. From that day Aquila was assumed to be rheumatic. It was Anisetta's act of faith.

Now, like Edward Gibbon, she sapped a faith by a solemn sneer.

*   *   *

By the time Aquila had recovered his breath from Anisetta's stinging insult, Lissom and Anisetta were a quarter of a mile down the road.

Aquila shook his fist after them.

"You musn't blame Anisetta," said Uncle Giorgio quickly. "She's not herself. She's under the influence of that man Lissom."

Aquila ground his teeth.

"When I get back to Monte Tauro, I shall show her that I'm no coward. I shall dive off The Rock in a December gale."

"Brava!" said Uncle Giorgio.

"But," went on Aquila, "I shall throw Anisetta in first."

"Fine!" said Uncle Giorgio. "No woman can resist being rescued from drowning."

"I may rescue her," said Aquila, "or I may not. That remains to be seen."

"So be it," said Uncle Giorgio. "But there is another way of showing your bravery, and we shall not have to wait until December. Nor," said Uncle Giorgio, marshalling his arguments, "will you have to do anything so foolhardy as diving to almost certain death in a winter sea."

"Well, what is it?" said Aquila, still gazing grimly down the empty road.

"Rescue your wife from that man!" said Uncle Giorgio. "Follow her! Give chase! And when you catch her, do not trouble any further to reason with Lissom. Hit him."

Aquila took his eyes away from the road. He looked hesitatingly at his uncle.

"Hit Lissom?" he said.

"Certainly," said Giorgio. "This is no trial marriage," he said waving his hand in the direction of the fleeing lovers. "This is no progressive sexual experiment. This is marriage by capture. This is a reversion to the Dark Ages."

The cry of 'Allah-i-Akbar!' could turn Mohammedans, effetely reclining by marble fountains among their womenfolk, into warriors that were the terror of Hindustan. 'This is a reversion to the Dark Ages,' though not so neat, is nowadays equally effective. There is no need to tell progressive people to go forward. But they are stirred to the core by a warning that we might be going back.

"You're right!" said Aquila, for the first time in his life agreeing without argument to something said by a member of his own family. "After them!"

Together they made a dash for the waiting taxi.

It will be seen that Aquila was subject to sudden changes of mind. First he cries 'Vengeance!' then he cries 'Reason!' and now he cries 'After them!' This may be bewildering but it is very Sicilian.

The intellectual taxi driver was sunk in meditation when Giorgio and Aquila leaped into his taxi, setting it rocking wildly on its springs.

"Quick," shouted Giorgio. "Five pounds if you catch the station-wagon!"

There had been times in Giorgio's life when a single shout of his had brought men left for dead to their feet to fire a last round at the Carabinieri. The taxi driver, who had never before heard such a noise come from a human throat, was so startled that for some half a mile he drove like a maniac.

Suddenly Aquila cried, "There they are!" and pointed to a dimly lit petrol station over some wide cross-roads. Beside a pump stood the station wagon. Behind it, a man in overalls was screwing the cap back on the petrol tank.

As their taxi hurtled towards the cross-roads, Giorgio and Aquila saw a hand come out of the driving window of the station wagon holding a currency note. The overalled man ran round, snatched it, touched his cap, and with a shuddering jump the station wagon drove off into the darkness.

"Drive for all you're worth," shouted Giorgio to the taxi driver. "Don't lose sight of them!"

The taxi, with its tyres and brakes screaming, came to a dead stop.

Aquila beat his head against the cushions.

"Go on, go *on*," he said almost in tears. "Go *on*."

"For God's sake what are we stopping for?" Uncle Giorgio demanded through the sliding window.

The taxi driver turned his intellectual face slowly round upon them. Equally slowly he pointed to the skies.

Aquila pressed his face against the glass, peering into the blackness. "What is it?" he asked the taxi driver almost hysterically. "What can you see?"

"Traffic lights," said the taxi driver and returned instantly to his meditations.

Uncle Giorgio, leaning out of the window, said:
"Look."

Aquila, following his glance, saw suspended by wires above the empty cross-roads a single unwinking red light.

"Jump them!" commanded Aquila, hammering on the window-frame.

Once more the taxi driver turned his educated face towards his fares.

"Half a mo' now, half a mo'," he said in a reasonable voice. "What would happen if everybody just ran over traffic lights every time they were in a hurry? I put it to you as intelligent men, what would happen? Chaos," he said, answering his own question. "That's what we'd have. Chaos. We don't want that, do we?"

"But there's not a car in bloody sight," said Aquila, losing in his agitation his usually remarkable grip on the English language.

"Nor a policeman," said Giorgio, looking quickly through each window and out of the small one at the back.

The taxi driver leaned ponderously out of his driving seat and slowly scrutinized the road.

"If my uncle says there's no policeman, you can take his word for it," said Aquila, testily. "He can smell them at two hundred yards."

The taxi driver resumed his normal position at the wheel.

"Ah!" he said, "but as foreigners, if you'll excuse the word, you wouldn't understand. Why do you think England is such a law-abiding place? Now I ask you, why is it?"

Giorgio and Aquila, their eyes fixed on the still-red light, shook their heads.

"I'll tell you," said the taxi driver. "It's because we obey the law *even when nobody's looking.*"

Giorgio and Aquila made no reply. The taxi driver joined them in studying the light. But whereas for his passengers the light stood for frustration, for the educated taxi driver it was merely an adjunct to further speculation, as bright objects are said to assist searchers after the Infinite.

"Besides," he said, "all this Rush and Tear. I don't hold with it. Wherever will it lead to?" he settled himself comfortably. He gave a little philosophical laugh. "People are always saying to me," he went on, " 'Hurry driver' 'Step on it, driver!' But I often say to myself, 'And supposing I *do* hurry. What are you going to do with all the time I've saved you?'

"You read that in a book," said Aquila sharply.

The taxi driver regarded him with the smile of a lecturer who has had an interrupter delivered into his hands.

"And what if I did?" he asked. "It just shows you that I've got time to read books. And why? Because I don't hold with Rush and Tear."

"The garage man is signalling something," said Uncle Giorgio.

The driver ignored him.

"Because why?" he said, pursuing his argument. "Because where is Rush and Tear getting us? That's what I want to know. Ho, yes, we're going faster all right," he said ironically. "But where are we going faster to?"

"I think the garage man says we're to come on," said Uncle Giorgio.

"Where has Rush and Tear got America?" said the taxi driver. "Look at them. Reno, Beauty Competitions. Boop-e-doop-boop," he said with a disconcerting flash of mime. "And where's that getting them? Lost Week-ends," he said grimly.

Uncle Giorgio tapped the driver on the shoulder.

"I don't want to interrupt your train of thought, but when a man points to a light and then makes a sign *so,*" said Uncle Giorgio waving his hands backwards and forwards in a plane level with the floor of the taxi, "would you think that he meant that the light was out of order?"

The taxi driver looked at Giorgio. Then he looked at the distant garage man, who was still gesticulating. Then he looked at the light. Finally, he let in his clutch.

"That's another thing," he said. "Machines. Where's all this depending on machines going to get us? Robots, that's what we're becoming. You mark my words."

But neither Aquila nor Giorgio did anything of the sort. They were too busy shouting to the garage hand to tell them where, if he knew, the station wagon was heading for.

*   *   *

The garage-hand said he couldn't rightly remember.

What he meant to say (he enlarged) was that he did not rightly know whether he ought to say where Professor Lissom was going to, seeing as how (he explained) it wasn't rightly his job to answer questions by some of his customers about other of his customers.

He didn't (he protested) want to disoblige *any* of his customers. He would like to answer the question, but what he wanted to know was (he concluded), Was it Right?

This is called the British character, and very fine it is—an unremitting search for moral perfection. It is a pity that Aquila did not, at the moment, appreciate it.

He said:

"For God's sake shut up, and let me explain. That man's stolen my wife! Is *that* right or isn't it? Don't answer. I know. It's a scandal. Now which way did they go?"

The garage-hand, overwhelmed by Aquila's violence, told him.

"Drive to the airport!" shouted Giorgio and slammed the taxi door.

*   *   *

Neither the taxi nor the driver moved.

"Drive to the airport!" shouted Giorgio again.

This time the taxi driver, with great deliberation, got down, came to the side of the taxi, opened the door and said:

"I'm a respectably married man."

Aquila and Giorgio, dumfounded, said nothing, waiting for him to go on.

He for his part remained, in the door, silent.

"Well," said Uncle Giorgio, when the silence had grown uncomfortable, "that's fine. See that your wife doesn't get mixed up with philosophers. And now, please drive us to the airport."

"That," said the taxi driver, "is what I will not do. I don't know what's going on; I don't *want* to know. But what I do know is as something's going on and what's going on isn't respectable. What I say is that you're a free man, if foreign,

and you've a right to go chasing women all over the country
if you wish to, but *not with me*. Am I right?" he appealed to
the garage-hand.

"Quite right," said the garage-hand. This also is part of
the British character, and this is also very fine—moral solidar-
ity in a crisis.

Aquila lost his head. He swore, he begged, he drew terrible
pictures of what would happen to his wife, he wept, he pleaded,
he threatened and he bawled. He spoke for at least five minutes
without stopping. But unfortunately he was so distraught that
he spoke entirely in Sicilian.

The taxi driver listened patiently. He did not understand
a word of what was being said. When Aquila's tirade was quite
finished the taxi driver said:

"I daresay you would, sir. But not in my taxi."

Aquila put his hands to his head and tugged fiercely at his
hair, incapable of saying another word.

Uncle Giorgio put his hand in his inside pocket.

The gun, however, was gone.

Uncle Giorgio remembered with dismay that he had given
it to Aquila. He thought for a moment of asking Aquila to
draw it. But one of his favorite sayings, roughly translated,
said that a woman and a gun both call for a firm hand. Observing Aquila's agitation, he gave up this plan and cast
around for another.

Now Uncle Giorgio was not intellectually proud. He
was willing to learn, even from his juniors. He therefore
very sensibly recalled Aquila's advice about handling the
English.

In less time than it takes to tell he had run through the
key-points of his knowledge of how to appeal to Anglo-Saxons.
He came to a decision.

"I feel," he said mildly, "there has been some mistake."

"A good many I should say," agreed the taxi driver, "but
other people's private affairs is none of my business."

"I mean," persisted Giorgio, "that you seem to think that
a woman is involved."

The taxi driver looked at the garage-hand. The garage-hand looked back at the taxi driver.

"Your friend said that that man had stolen his wife, didn't he?"

"Wife?" said Uncle Giorgio, marvellously puzzled.

"Wife," said the taxi driver.

"Oh-ho-ho, I *see* where we've all gone wrong," said Uncle Giorgio, his face lighting up. "My nephew said, 'He's stolen my *life*.' Not wife. *Life*. It's his Italian way of talking. He loves it more than his life, I should say."

"Loves what?" asked the taxi driver.

"Anisetta," said Uncle Giorgio, shaking his head sadly.

"Who's Anisetta?" asked the garage-hand.

"A dog," said Uncle Giorgio.

"A *dog?*" said the taxi driver and the garage-hand together.

"A priceless, beautiful borzoi," said Uncle Giorgio: adding, inspired, "A Sicilian borzoi. There are only two other specimens in the world. Both are in France and both, like poor Anisetta, were *kidnapped*."

"Kidnapping dogs?" said the taxi driver in a horrified voice.

Giorgio nodded.

"There's a horribly cruel underground traffic going on in them," he said. "Didn't you know? Smuggling gold and jewels has become too difficult. Pictures can be traced. But a man can walk aboard a plane with a dog and who'd ask questions? When they get them to the other side and they're out of quarantine, they *do* things to them, so their own mothers wouldn't recognize them."

"The poor little devils," broke out the taxi driver, passionately.

"They're kept in a sack most of the time," said Giorgio. "You must have seen it in the back of the station wagon," he added to the garage-hand.

"I did see something," said the garage-hand. "If only I'd have known."

"That's what everybody says," remarked Giorgio sombrely.

"It's like horses," said the taxi driver. "They used to send poor horses to Belgium. That was stopped."

"Now they send poor innocent dogs," said Giorgio.

"They used to pole-axe the horses," said the taxi driver with a shudder.

"What they do to the dogs I don't know," went on Giorgio. "But I can guess."

The taxi driver swung round on the garage-hand.

"Well, what are you standing there for, shaking your head," he suddenly shouted. "You've got a telephone, haven't you? Well, warn the police to stop him at the airport. Tell them to get out the Flying Squad. Get cracking, man." He turned back to his passengers. He patted Aquila on the shoulder.

"Bear up," he said. "This is England. They can't get away with that sort of thing here."

Before Aquila could answer he found himself on his back on the floor, with Uncle Giorgio on top of him, while the taxi, leaping forward so quickly that it seemed the taxi driver had not so much started it as set spurs to its flanks, careered down the road towards the airport.

Uncle Giorgio picked himself up.

"*Ecco!*" he said, which means Lo and Behold.

*   *   *

As they neared the airport Aquila, clinging to a side-strap, said:

"Uncle, why are you crossing yourself?"

"I am thinking of the English, Aquila."

"Are you praying for them, Uncle?"

"No," said Giorgio. "It is not necessary. God is not only merciful to sinners, He even takes pity on the wise. He sends them," said Uncle Giorgio reverently, "just a little mad."

CHAPTER VII

THE EXISTENTIAL MARQUIS

Anisetta stood on a balcony with Professor Lissom and saw Paris for the first time in her life.

She was at first a little disappointed to find so many houses, because she had made up her mind from a study of travel posters that all Parisians lived in the Eiffel Tower.

Lissom stood by her side, holding her hand, but a little absently. His manner had been preoccupied ever since they arrived.

He pulled himself together.

"Well!" he said, "your first sight of Paris! I envy you. Don't you think it is very beautiful?"

"It is very well planned," said Anisetta cautiously.

"But there is more than planning," said Lissom, "there is an atmosphere, an indescribable something that is *France.*"

He said this rather less than convincingly because France and particularly Paris had always seemed to him a rather dull place in an earnest sort of way. This lapse of taste he accounted for by the fact that his ancestry was not wholly British, one of his grandmothers having come from Spain. He had another un-English trait, as we shall see. This second trait he could not conceal. The first, he could.

"Do you know what Sir Austen Chamberlain once said about France?" he asked Anisetta.

"No," said Anisetta. "Who is Sir Austen Chamberlain?"

"He was a great English statesman who wore an eye-glass and was a Knight of the Garter."

"Oh," said Anisetta. "Well, what did he say?" She looked critically at Sacré Coeur, thinking it looked too white and

86

much smaller than St. Peter's looked in the pictures people sent her from Rome.

"He said that he loved France as he loved a woman."

A silence fell between them.

"Isn't that a wonderful thing to say?"

"Well," said Anisetta, "it all depends on how he loved a woman."

Finding nothing to reply to this, Lissom fell once more into an abstraction.

A little later, while they were sitting in a café and Anisetta was enjoying the Spring sunshine, he said, suddenly, "Why *dogs?*"

A little later, while they were sitting in the same café, and Anisetta was admiring the Spring fashions, Lissom, who had said nothing in the interval, remarked, with a puzzled air:

" 'Pas des chiens,' I told them. 'Pas des chiens de tout.' Of course my French isn't any good, but that doesn't account for all the fuss. What about Birmingham? What about the C.I.D. man who held up the plane? 'No dogs,' I kept saying. But nobody believed me. Why?"

Anisetta did not know. Once more Lissom fell into an abstraction, and one even more profound.

Half an hour later they were looking at the Venus de Milo.

Anisetta yawned. She plucked Lissom's sleeve.

"Frankie," she said, "I don't want to grumble, because I know you aim to please me but I think you have made a mistake. I've heard it said that when men come to Paris they like to see women with no clothes on, but with women it is the other way about. Can't we go and see a fashion parade?"

"My dear," said Lissom, recalling himself with a start, "anything you please. Of course. Let us go straight away."

In a short time they were seated in very comfortable chairs watching a procession of mannequins and for the first time Anisetta saw why people make so much fuss about the charms of foreign travel. Lissom, pleased with Anisetta's enthusiasm, became quite lively.

Unfortunately he was seated next to an American matron, and at the feet of the American matron sat a dog. The dog being exceedingly small, Lissom did not see it for quite ten minutes. During this time Anisetta, to her relief, found Lissom more entertaining than at any stage of her escapade since they arrived at Birmingham airport. He repeated, inimitably, the most successful of his quiz-quips about women's fashions.

Then he trod on the dog, quite lightly, but the dog yapped. The American matron quickly hushed the dog to silence. She smiled in a neighborly fashion at Lissom. Lissom did not respond. He was staring fixedly at the dog. He was once more lost in abstraction. This time it was so severe that he spoke aloud.

"It is incomprehensible," he said. "Why should they all be so sure that I had a dog somewhere concealed?" This remark had coincided with the announcement by the mistress of ceremonies of a particularly striking frock. His next remark, although still made to himself, came out in the midst of a deep silence.

"I do not even like dogs," he said.

This, of course, is the second lapse that was promised at the beginning of this chapter, and must be put down to his grandmother who came from Spain.

"I think they are stupid, servile, bad-smelling and low-minded. As I said to the man from the Sûreté, the only reason I would take a dog in a plane is to drop it into the middle of the English Channel."

He remembered indignantly how he had been locked in a bare room in the Paris airport for half an hour while he was being interrogated. Though still looking at the little dog, he therefore said this last sentence with flashing eyes.

The American matron, hearing Lissom talking of dropping dogs from planes, screamed. Her dog began yapping furiously. Lissom, startled, trod on the dog's tail. The dog snapped at Lissom's ankle, and Lissom instinctively kicked it (I say instinctively, not because it is natural for an Englishman to kick a small dog, in any circumstances, but because of Lissom's grandmother who came from Spain).

This convinced the American matron that she was in the presence of a sadist with a bent for the cruel destruction of dogs. She gathered her dog up in her arms, and raising her voice above its volley of yaps, demanded that the man be removed.

Few people can make a public scene more effectively than an outraged American matron, except opera singers, and opera singers are hampered by having to be careful not to strain their throats. This particular American matron had no such check upon her capabilities.

The mistress of ceremonies soon saw she was faced with the choice of either abandoning the dress parade or throwing Lissom out. Calculating the price of Anisetta's frock with an expert eye, and comparing it with the small fortune it must have cost to clothe and be-jewel the woman with the dog, she asked Lissom to be so good as to leave.

Anisetta was by this time in a very bad temper, as what woman would not be, having been snatched away from the middle of a Parisian dress-show?

Lissom, alarmed by the blackness of her looks as they walked down the street, determined that it was high time he showed some gallantry. He hailed a taxi, and, with some mystery, gave the driver instructions in an undertone.

Some time later Anisetta found herself sitting beside Lissom on a seat in one of the most beautiful and secluded parts of the Bois de Boulogne.

Anisetta's had temper yielded a few shades of blackness. She thought the trees lovely. Lissom kissed her.

Anisetta sighed and leaned her head on Lissom's shoulder. Lissom kissed her hair.

Lissom took her chin and tilted her face up to his. He looked deep into her eyes. Then, slowly an expression of delight came shining in his own.

For a moment Anisetta feared that he was going to say, "Happy, darling?"

He did not. What he did say was, "I've got it! They mistook me for a King's Messenger."

Bewildered, Anisetta said, "What is a King's Messenger?"

"He is a man who takes important messages for the British Government. It all fits. They wear a badge. It's a silver dog!"

"Dogs!" said Anisetta, clenching her fist. "Always dogs!"

"Yes," Lissom swept on. "They were expecting a messenger who looked like me and when they saw that I was without my badge, they were worried. So when they kept on asking me about a dog, they expected me to make some secret sign to show that I was bona-fide but had changed my suit in a hurry. It *was* a greyhound that they were talking about, wasn't it?"

"No," said Anisetta, and her voice trembled.

"No? Then what was it?"

"I don't remember. I don't care," said Anisetta. "I don't give a damn about anything to do with dogs. I hope they all catch rabies and bite one another to death until there is only one dog left in the whole wide world, and I hope that the last thing he does before he drops dead is to bite you."

She burst into tears.

Lissom, most alarmed, did his best to apologize.

"But you must understand," he finished, "that it's the sort of thing that *worries* a man."

"The only thing that ought to be worrying you now is whether I love you enough to let you go to bed with me," sobbed Anisetta. "I thought you said passion was the most important thing in the world."

"Oh, it is, it is," said Lissom hastily. "It's one of Nature's great imperatives."

"Well, then," said Anisetta. She took his handkerchief out of his breast pocket and blew her nose.

"But you see, Nature is governed by cause and effect. That is also one of the guiding principles of my life. If I see an effect I believe it has a cause. And what is more, I believe that Man's unaided reason can discover that cause, given time."

Anisetta put her head back on his shoulder.

"Oh, yes," she said, "I agree. I like men to be dignified. Go on talking."

"But you don't want to be bored with philosophy," said Lissom.

"Yes, I do. It sounds so funny when you talk; the way it rumbles on your chest I mean."

"Well," said Lissom, "I believe in an orderly Universe. I don't believe in miracles. I don't believe in angels; I don't believe in demons. I believe in the laws of cause and effect. When I see an effect, I say, 'What is the cause?' I do not believe the Universe is mad. So when half a dozen uniformed men start questioning me about a dog, it's not that I don't love you any more, its just that—"

But he got no further because his voice was drowned by a great wail from Anisetta.

"I want to go back to my hu-hu-husband!" she cried, and tears poured down her cheeks.

With that, she jumped to her feet and ran blindly down the avenue. Lissom ran after her crying:

"Anisetta, Anisetta! Come back!"

But Anisetta, still running, only said:

"Aquila! Aquila. My boo-hoo-utiful Aquila. Where are you?" Between them they made enough disturbance to attract the attention not only of several passers-by, but also of a gendarme.

Being too late, and too much of a gentleman to tackle Anisetta, the gendarme tackled Lissom.

"Nom du chien!" exclaimed the gendarme. "What goes on here?"

Lissom, hearing this, went white to the lips and stood like a man who has come face to face with the Powers of Darkness.

*   *   *

Anisetta hailed a taxi, and her hotel having an Italian name, fortunately she remembered it.

When the taxi was on its way, Anisetta rummaged in her

hand-bag taking out a powder compact and a medallion stamped with the picture of Sant'Agata.

She laid the compact aside for the moment, and clutching the medallion in her right hand said:

"Blessed Sant'Agata I am a bad girl and I have sinned-exceedingly-in-thought-word-and-deed and the priest was quite right I should stick to the man he married me to because one man is just like another and they all have bees in their bonnet and if it comes to bees I'd rather have Reason and Civilization and Progress than dogs so send me back my husband blessed Sant'Agata and I promise you a candle on the first Friday of every month worldwithoutendamen."

With that she kissed the medallion, put it away in her bag, and since Sant'Agata has been looking after Sicilians for the last one thousand seven hundred years, Anisetta felt so certain that everything would be all right that she was able to re-make-up her face.

The taxi put her down at her hotel, the hall-porter paid the taxi, Anisetta walked into the hotel, and there, propped against a telephone was a telegram. It said:

"To Mrs. Pina Morales, passenger aboard Charter Plane GB-X231."

And somebody had crossed out the name of the Parisian airport and put the name of the hotel which Lissom had given the passport man.

In a moment Anisetta had torn it open and, ignoring the message, had gone straight to the name of the sender.

"YOUR LOVING HUSBAND AQUILA," it said.

"Thank you," said Anisetta simply.

The hall-porter bowed.

Anisetta ignored him. She had been speaking to Sant' Agata, who she knew would be hovering above her to see that everything was all right.

"It is a pleasure," said the hall-porter.

Sant'Agata, who is Sicilian and therefore as polite as any Frenchman, said, Anisetta had no doubt, "Prego," which means the same thing.

She folded the telegram together again and promised herself that she would read it all by herself in her room in case she was so happy she made a fool of herself.

On the way up in the lift she told herself that never, never again would she criticize her husband.

Walking along the corridor she admitted to herself that sending telegrams flying after her was some improvement on Aquila's previous conduct and showed some signs that he had decided to behave like a husband should.

But while the page-boy fiddled with her key in the lock of her room she could not help pointing out to herself that Aquila had been brought to his senses by the fact that she had taken things into her own hands.

When the page-boy finally got the door open and Anisetta was inside the room, she said to herself that if Aquila thought that a few loving words and an apology in a telegram were going to make her come running back with her tail between her legs, well then, all that she could say was that he would have to think again.

When she had locked the door against the possible return of Lissom, taken off her hat, scratched her head a little, and found a chair to sit in, she had made up her mind to treat protestations of love and repentance with objectivity, as became a woman who had asserted herself, once and for all, as the one who knew best.

She unfolded the telegram and smoothed it on her knee.

2PRS 37/10 BIRMINGHAM. 52/2.23. 14.21.
PROFONDAMENTE COLPITO LISSOM RIFIUTASI DISCUTERE RAZIONALMENTE NOSTRA CONTROVERSIA STOP MIA FEDE IN PROGRESSIVISMO LISSOM GRAVEMENTE SCOSSA MA NON PERDUTE TUTTE SPERANZE STOP PROFITTA SOGGIORNO PARIGI VISITANDO CATTEDRALE NOTRE DAME UNICA CATTEDRALE AL MONDO DEDICATA UNA VOLTA DEA RAGIONE ARRIVEDERCI PRESTO TUA AQUILA.

That is to say:

DEEPLY DISTRESSED LISSOM UNWILLING DISCUSS MAT-

TERS IN RATIONAL MANNER STOP FAITH LISSOMS PRO-
GRESSIVENESS GRAVELY SHAKEN BUT KEEPING OPEN
MIND STOP WHILE IN PARIS DO NOT MISS OPPORTUNITY
VISIT NOTRE DAME ONLY CATHEDRAL IN WORLD ONCE
DEDICATED TO GODDESS OF REASON SEE YOU SOON
YOUR LOVING HUSBAND AQUILA.

*　　　*　　　*

She threw the telegram on the floor. She stamped on it.
She picked it up and crumpled it into a small ball.

But she went to Notre Dame. Perhaps it was because she
was at heart a good wife and did, when she possibly could, what
her husband told her. Perhaps it was Sant'Agata again. In any
case she went.

Outside the great door she stopped, and craning her neck
backwards, looked up at the cathedral. It was very big. It
was probably not much smaller than St. Peter's. But the men
who built it seemed to Anisetta to have had only one idea, and
that was—spikes. Now really good church-builders, in Anisetta's opinion, always had several ideas, all different, so that
everything looked lovely and wavy. She preferred churches to
be wavy.

It can be seen from this that she was no judge of the outside of churches. Any English or American schoolgirl could
have told her more about them than she would ever know. But
then, she could have told them something about the insides that
few of the schoolgirls know. The insides are used—and especially in Sicily—for the worship of God. So Anisetta wasted no
more time but went straight through the door and dipped her
fingers in the stoup of holy water.

A man with a badge came up to her and said something
which she did not understand.

"Do you speak Italian?" she asked.

"Certainly," he said, and did so, pointing to his guide's
badge.

"Good," said Anisetta, "I want to buy a candle."

The guide bowed and pointed to an old woman sitting just

within the doorway. In front of her she had bundles of candles of all sizes. Anisetta chose one with great care and the guide saved her from paying one hundred times its price, because she, as yet, was not familiar with the French currency notes, even if those in her handbag had been manufactured by one of her relatives by marriage.

"Thank you," said Anisetta to the guide. "I shall not need you any more."

"But signorina . . ." protested the guide.

"I have been well brought up. I am quite capable of finding my way around a church," said Anisetta.

But she was not. The churches in which she had been well brought up did not climb sharply half-way to heaven and bend over at the top to hold in what seemed to be a cloud of mist. Anisetta's churches were filled with light and a riot of boy-angels. The chapels of the churches she knew were not sudden glades in a forest of stone pillars. They were more like big bow windows with a saint in glory instead of a window pane and none of them was difficult to find. As for the statues themselves Anisetta's were lively and smiling and went vigorously about their holy business. These were all tall and thin as though drawn out with yearning; and none of them smiled.

She heard chanting, but it was muddled by the echo until it sounded like a threat. She saw a gold-coped priest walk past a pillar. But the priest looked much too small and the pillar gloomily vast. And there was no yellow window making its own sunshine, whatever the weather. This, being a Sicilian, she missed most of all.

She looked back and was relieved to find the guide still standing where she had left him.

"Excuse me," she said, "but could you direct me to the chapel of the Goddess of Reason?"

The guide looked bewildered.

"Are you sure you have the right place?" he asked.

"Of course," said Anisetta. "My husband sent me a telegram and my husband is never wrong."

She dug into her hand-bag, found the telegram, still

crumpled into a ball, and smoothing it out gave it to the guide to read.

But his Italian did not stretch so far, and he looked around him for help.

He darted off and Anisetta saw him fall into conversation with a man who was standing in the middle of the nave with his arms (and this Anisetta thought odd for a man in a church) tightly folded across his breast. From time to time as the guide talked to him, the man shot baleful glances at the high altar.

After a few moments the guide came trotting back, the man following him at a more elegant pace.

"This is the very gentleman to help you," said the guide.

Anisetta looked at him. He was exquisitely dressed in silver grey, matching his greying temples; he had a long nose, long eyes, a long mouth, long hands ending in long fingers. And he was very short. He appeared therefore like the cartoons of politicians in which everything above the waist is perfectly proportioned, but below that the artist has drawn two spindle legs that could not possibly support such a torso. But this man's legs did support him, as is the way with many Frenchmen.

He gazed at Anisetta for a moment with his long eyes and then raised a pair of long eyebrows.

"Madame," he said, "*Signora,* I shall be charmed to put myself entirely at your service. The guide, who is, in a way, an old friend of mine, tells me that your husband . . ." He paused. "It *was* your husband?" he asked.

"Yes," said Anisetta, "it was my husband."

His long mouth drooped slightly.

"Exactly," he said. "Your husband, I am told, sent you a telegram? It *was* a telegram?"

"Yes," said Anisetta, "it was a telegram."

His long mouth smiled a long smile.

"Then of course your husband is not in Paris?"

"No," said Anisetta. "My husband of course is not in Paris. If we were together he would not send me telegrams, would he?"

"Oh!" said the man, "it has happened. Indeed yes. But not of course to men married to so enchanting a wife as you. You are sightseeing?"

"Not exactly," said Anisetta, determined to bring the conversation back to the matter in hand (although she found the Frenchman's manners most agreeable). "I want to offer a candle to the Goddess of Reason."

"Indeed?" said the man, and looked her up and down for all the world (thought Anisetta) as though he were checking up to see that she was dressed decently for the ceremony. Seemingly he found that she was, for he bowed his long body on its short legs and said:

"I shall be delighted to help you."

With that he tipped the guide and sent him away.

"Please come with me," he said, and taking Anisetta's arm, steered her between some pillars into a quiet aisle.

"First," he said, "allow me to introduce myself." He held towards Anisetta a card as long and thin as his fingers.

Anisetta read, with some surprise,

Le Marquis de Sallotte

and over the middle of the name floated the picture of a tiny coronet.

Now Anisetta, being an Italian, was very impressed by titles. They are much used in Italy and are almost essential for any sort of social standing. In fact the demand for titles in Italy is so brisk that they are sold at very reasonable rates. Thus where an English girl would have giggled (because all the English believe that the English invented titles and the world outside merely copies them) and where an American girl would have invited him to dinner on the spot (because all Americans think that foreign nobility do not get enough to eat), Anisetta made him a respectful bow and while hoping he was a gentleman, was quite certain that he was rich.

"I am Signora Morales," said Anisetta. "I come from Monte Tauro. I am surprised you are a Marquis. Aquila told me that all the French aristocrats had their heads cut off."

"Madame," said the Marquis, "I will confess to you that we are not so old a family. We had our title from Napoleon the Third."

"I see," said Anisetta, "that was after they had cut off everybody's head, was it?"

"Some time after, Madame. But I hope you will not think any less of me for that."

"Oh no," Anisetta answered quickly. "I think it's a very sensible time to get a title. Like not buying a puppy until it's over distemper age."

"Ah!" said the Marquis admiringly, "I see that you are a woman of the world."

Being told that she was a woman of the world reminded Anisetta that she had received a telegram.

She gave it to the Marquis.

He found one of the innumerable loose chairs that clutter a Catholic church and set it for Anisetta to sit on. With a genuflection in the direction of an impossibly distant high altar, Anisetta sat down.

Lest it should seem surprising that Anisetta should be behaving in a church as though she were at home, I should say in her defense that, indeed, she was at home in it. She had spent three-quarters of an hour in it every Sunday of her life. Had she been born elsewhere but in Italy, no doubt she would have gone to church far less often and behaved, when she did, with most edifying reverence.

The Marquis read the telegram with attention.

"I regret," he said at length, "that you will not find the Goddess of Reason here."

"But that is impossible. My husband could not have made a mistake. He says the church of Notre Dame."

"That means the church of Our Lady," said the Marquis.

"Does it?" said Anisetta, "I did not know because I do not speak French. Well, then," she said rising, "there we are." She began to walk up the church. "Who could be a better Goddess of Reason than Our Lady?"

"Why do you think that?" asked the Marquis, following her.

"Why?" asked Anisetta in astonishment. "Don't you? Aren't you a Catholic?"

"Alas, no longer," said the Marquis.

"Then why do you stand in the middle of the church?" asked Anisetta, adding, "with your arms folded?"

"That is a long story," said the Marquis sadly, "which I hope I shall soon have the privilege of telling you."

They had come to a chapel that was ablaze with candles. Anisetta gave hers to a sacristan and watched him light it.

"Well," she said at last, simply, "when the angel brought the good tiding to Our Lady, what did Our Lady say?"

Anisetta folded her hands and in the soft-running Latin that Italians use she said the beginning of the *Magnificat*.

"And what could be more reasonable than that?" she asked.

*   *   *

When they came out of the Cathedral (and the Marquis had accompanied her as though it was the most natural thing in the world), Anisetta said:

"Now you must tell me why you stood looking so black, and with your arms folded, in church."

"Madame," said the Marquis with a beautiful smile, "if they would win ten more minutes of your charming company, I would tear out the secrets of my soul and lay them at your feet."

Anisetta said:

"Well, you can see me to my hotel if you like."

The Sicilians, though talkative, are not given to flowers of speech.

"Madame, I shall be delighted," said the Marquis, and, for a moment looked it. But an acquaintance of the Marquis passed him, and raised his hat. The Marquis raised his own hat, and bowed slightly in the direction of his friend with an expression of such ferocity that Anisetta fell back a pace in alarm.

The next instant the Marquis had turned to her and asked: "Now, which road shall we take for your hotel?"

His expression was all warmth, sunshine and happiness.

Anisetta, disconcerted, fumbled a little in telling him where she lived. With the greatest charm of manner the Marquis sorted out her replies, and set out towards her hotel with a bouncing step.

Turning a corner, they met another friend of the Marquis. The friend raised his hat, the Marquis raised his. Both men regarded each other for a moment with expressions of the bitterest despair. They said a word or two in French. Then they went on their ways.

"Bad news?" said Anisetta.

"What?" asked the Marquis, smiling suddenly, as he had done before. "No, not that I know of."

"Oh!" said Anisetta. "I thought perhaps that your friend that you just passed told you something that made you unhappy."

"Henri? Good heavens no!" said the Marquis, but affably. "He merely said 'Good morning.'"

"I see," said Anisetta, but for the next few minutes she watched him narrowly from the corner of her eye.

It happened a third time, but even more mysteriously. The Marquis had launched into an amusing story about an experience of his when he had last been in Anisetta's hotel and was laughing gaily as he told it. Still laughing, he touched his hat to a third friend. The friend in turn touched his own hat but with an expression of such misery that Anisetta felt that she was not walking beside a happy (if changeable) Marquis, but his hearse.

The Marquis caught this look, hesitated in his step, and to Anisetta's astonishment, blushed deeply down to his collar. He then composed his face as best he could, drew down the corners of his mouth, muttered a gloomy 'Good morning,' and passed on.

But he was clearly put out. He took up the story again, but

with less ease, and he examined the passers-by warily, as though wishing to be forewarned of any other friends who might be coming his way.

He brought his story to an end.

Anisetta laughed politely and said:

"That is most amusing but it does not tell me why you stood in church looking angry with your arms folded, nor why all your friends are so unhappy, nor why you think so badly of them. Now you must keep your promise and explain."

The Marquis stopped dead.

"Madame," he said, very seriously.

Anisetta stopped in surprise beside him.

"Yes?" she said.

The Marquis' serious look grew even deeper.

"Before I accompany you any further on your walk to your hotel," he said, "I think I owe it to you to tell you that I am an Existentialist."

Anisetta was rather surprised, but quickly recovered. She said:

"Oh well, that doesn't matter really, because I'm not going to ask you up to my room or anything. And I don't suppose you'd be an Exy-whatever-it-is in public. You look too much of a gentleman."

Still serious, the Marquis thought this over.

"You mistake me," he said. "Existentialism has nothing to do with sex. It is a philosophy of living."

"I don't think it's much of a philosophy of living if it's got nothing to do with sex," Anisetta told him.

"How wise you are," said the Marquis admiringly.

"Maybe," said Anisetta, none too pleased.

"As *well* as beautiful," said the Marquis.

"Maybe," said Anisetta again, but very pleased indeed, because no woman objects to being called intelligent provided she is assured that it has done no harm to her looks. "But we're getting off the point again. Why are you so gloomy, off and on?"

"Because I am an Existentialist," said the Marquis.

"Can't you go for a holiday or something and get over it?" asked Anisetta.

"Yes," admitted the Marquis, "but then I would be dreadfully out of fashion."

"But are you *really* unhappy?" asked Anisetta.

"No," said the Marquis. "As a matter of fact I am by temperament a remarkably sanguine man. But it is necessary to be as it is necessary to be," he said, and for the fourth time raised his hat to a friend with an expression of profound despair.

"Well, of all the silly fashions!" said Anisetta, as the Marquis guided her across a broad square. "And I thought only women made fools of themselves in order to be up to date."

"Women very sensibly make fools of themselves over fashions in clothes," said the Marquis, when they were safe on the other side. "A woman may make herself look like a monster but she still thinks like a human being, whereas I am afraid that men are stupid enough to have fashions in what they think."

"I find it very difficult," he complained after a pause. "But I do try to remember that life has no meaning and God does not exist."

"Was *that* what you were doing in church?" asked Anisetta.

"Yes," said the Marquis, "I was practicing."

At this they turned into some pretty gardens where children were playing among statues and flowers.

Anisetta admired the scene for a while and then said as an after-thought:

"I wonder that you weren't struck dead on the spot."

"I think that that would be most unfair," said the Marquis. "After all, why should I be singled out? I am a very bad Existentialist."

"Why?" asked Anisetta.

They sat on a seat under a tree.

"Because I cannot help feeling that the world is rather a jolly place," said the Marquis. As he said this he heaved so deep a sigh and looked so very sad that Anisetta was quite touched.

"Does that get you into trouble with all the other Exy-what's-its?" asked Anisetta sympathetically.

"Yes," said the Marquis, "particularly with my mother. She is a very distinguished woman who runs a salon. You probably do not know what a salon is, so I will tell you. It is a place where clever and important people come and drink and talk."

Anisetta clapped her hands.

"Oh!" she said, "how lucky your mother is! I have always longed to run a salon. I would have tables outside with umbrellas and serve *cassata alla Siciliana* every day, so I could have some myself instead of having to wait until somebody gets married."

The Marquis crossed his short legs and looked at Anisetta with his long eyes.

"The longer I know you," he said, "the more I feel we were destined to be the most wonderful friends. I adore *cassata alla Siciliana*. It is one of the greatest pleasures in life. At least," he added, pulling himself up, "if there *were* any pleasures in life."

"Is your mother an Exy-you-know-what?" asked Anisetta.

"Oh yes," said the Marquis, "and a very prominent one. In fact Existentialism practically started in her salon."

"She must have served bad refreshments," said Anisetta. "When my sister was married we had some awful Asti Spumante, and everybody burst into tears."

"Existentialists do not burst into tears," said the Marquis. "It would not be so bad if they did. Then it would be like the Russians. I have had some very happy evenings with Russians in Paris. They like me because I am very emotional. I always cry at the sad parts in pictures. But Existentialists do not approve of crying. They face life with a grim smile. It is very awkward for me because, as you may have noticed, when I smile I am not at all grim. And as for facing life, I live on an income which my mother allows me. She is very disappointed in me. She is always leaving books by M. Jean-Paul Sartre in my way, hoping I will learn the facts of life, but I find them very hard going."

Anisetta leaned over the back of the seat, picked a flower, and in the Sicilian fashion, put the stalk in her mouth.

"What do they say?" she said, chewing.

"It's difficult to explain simply, but I'll try," said the Marquis. "It goes something like this: take anything."

"Anything?"

"Anything."

"Well," said Anisetta. "Let's take a cow."

"Very well," said the Marquis, "take a cow. The Existentialists do not usually take a cow; they prefer to take a table. Or sometimes a loose woman. But let *us* take a cow. Now, a cow *exists.*"

"Yes, it does, doesn't it?" said Anisetta. "I do see that."

"I don't think you should see it quite so quickly," said the Marquis. "Existence is really a most complicated theory, I believe, and you cannot understand it until you have read at least three books."

"How much do the books cost?" asked Anisetta.

The Marquis told her.

"That is a lot of money to pay for learning that a cow exists. I do not think that life can be very grim for the man who wrote those books. In fact, if he sells any number at all, I think it must be very rosy. But let us get back to my cow."

"Your cow, then," said the Marquis, "exists. It doesn't know *why* it exists."

"It doesn't ask," said Anisetta.

"No," said the Marquis thoughtfully. And then after a pause. "As a matter of fact, I am very fond of cows."

"So am I," said Anisetta.

"As much, or more than *cassata alla Siciliana?*" asked the Marquis.

Anisetta thought.

"A little bit less," she decided.

"Just what I think," said the Marquis happily. "We *do* get on well together."

"Yes," said Anisetta, "but you are getting off the point. Just because you have proved that cows exist, it doesn't follow that life has no meaning."

The Marquis sighed.

"That's what I always say," he complained, "and Mother gets *so* angry." His face suddenly brightened. "You don't by any chance know what the meaning of Life is, do you? Because if you do, that would be wonderful. When Mother threatens to cut off my allowance, as she does on the first of every month, I could rap back at her quick and say, 'But Mother, Life has a meaning: it is such and such,' and she would look at me dumfounded, and say 'Joel'—that's my name—'Joel, I am proud of you.' You don't happen to know, do you?"

Anisetta thought. The Marquis waited, all suspense.

"No," said Anisetta.

"I see," said the Marquis. "Pity."

"The trouble with you," said Anisetta sternly, "is that you jump to conclusions. When I said 'No,' I didn't just mean, 'No, I don't know,' I meant 'No, I don't know and I *know* that I don't know.' That's what you ought to say to your mother. She'd have no answer to that."

"Well," said the Marquis politely, "not if I said it, for instance, when she was just moving off in a train bound for Constantinople. But normally my mother has an answer for everything. And that's where the trouble starts, because I haven't. I can't keep my end up."

"It's really quite simple," said Anisetta. "It's like there being five continents."

"Is it now?" said the Marquis, admiringly. "You know, I would almost say that that is a remark to which even my mother would not have a reply. Why is it like the five continents?"

"I shall tell you, but don't hurry me," said Anisetta. "What are the five continents?"

"Europe, to begin with," said the Marquis.

"And Africa," said Anisetta.

"America," said the Marquis.

"North and South," said Anisetta.

"North and South," agreed the Marquis.

"Asia," said Anisetta. "And that makes four because North and South only count as one."

"Agreed," said the Marquis.

"And what's the fifth?" asked Anisetta.

"Australia."

"Well there you are, you see," said Anisetta. "I didn't know that. I never do know it. I never can remember."

"I shouldn't think it matters," said the Marquis reassuringly. "Australia's a long way away."

"That's not the point," said Anisetta impatiently. "The point is that I don't only forget the name of the place, I don't know anything about it at all. But that doesn't mean that I say it isn't there. You see what I mean? Australia is Life."

"In a very limited way, I should say," said the Marquis, doubtfully.

"No, I mean that Australia is just the same as Life and what it's about. I don't know, but I don't make up theories about it. I just say I don't know."

The Marquis' eyes lit up.

"And you don't ask questions?"

"No," agreed Anisetta.

"You mean you're just like the . . . the domestically useful animal which we took at the beginning of this argument?" said the Marquis with enthusiasm.

"The cow?" asked Anisetta.

"Well, yes," said the Marquis.

"If you put it in that way," said Anisetta, doubtfully, "I suppose, yes."

"My dear young lady," said the Marquis fervently, "I would not dream of putting it in any way but in your own illuminating words. Do you mind if I make a few notes? I can run over them on the first of the month. It will give me great confidence."

"By all means," said Anisetta, and the Marquis, taking out a small note-book bound at the corners with gold clasps, wrote diligently with a gold-cased pencil.

"Know that I don't know . . ." he muttered as he wrote. And then, "Cow."

Anisetta, catching this, said:

"It's not exactly like the cow, because a cow doesn't do anything about anything."

The Marquis stopped writing. "But you do?" he asked, his pencil poised expectantly above his notebook.

"Yes," said Anisetta. "I don't ask whether life has any meaning. I just leave it to Sant'Agata, and Sant'Agata leaves it to God. And God knows, because he started it."

The Marquis closed his note-book.

"I could not be more disappointed," he said, and looked it.

"Whyever not?" asked Anisetta.

"Because there is no God."

"Do you believe that?"

"Please, dear lady, I have been perfectly frank about my position. It is not so much what I believe, it is what my mother believes, and particularly on the first of the month. And my mother believes that there is no God because M. Jean-Paul Sartre says so."

"And this gentleman is very gloomy, I suppose."

"He's a busy man," said the Marquis cautiously. "But he suffers from *angst,* of course."

"Poor man," said Anisetta sympathetically. "What is *angst?*"

"It means that he is always very anxious."

"I should jolly well think he would be," said Anisetta vigorously.

"You mean that he ought to expect to be struck by lightning?"

"No. I wouldn't be surprised if before he's much older he'd regard a thunderbolt as a mercy. If he doesn't believe in God he doesn't believe that God decides and that means he has to decide everything for himself. And *that* means that he's God himself," said Anisetta.

The Marquis regarded her with open-mouthed admiration.

"That's what *he* says," he replied.

"Of course he does. It's like my white dress, isn't it?"

"Yes," said the Marquis reverently. "I do not know why, but after Australia, I have faith." He opened his notebook. "Please continue," he said.

"You needn't put all of it down, but I had a white dress for my first Communion and when my mother was fitting it on me one day just before Easter, I ran out to show it to the other girls, although my mother had told me not to, and I played some games and got it dirty. My mother was awfully cross and she spanked me. So I was cross too, and when next day I went to my catechism lesson with the Cappuccini—they're nuns— I said I didn't want to have anything to do with the silly old church and anyway I didn't believe in the Ten Commandments."

"How precocious," said the Marquis. "Neither does M. Sartre."

"The nun took it quite quietly," Anisetta went on. "All she said was, 'Well, Anisetta my dear, if you don't believe in God's Commandments, then you'd better think out some for yourself: only of course they'll have to be commandments for all the other girls as well, so you'd better talk it over with them first.' So I did and it was awful and I got a headache. It was all right at first, because we all agreed to cut out one of them."

"Which was that?"

" 'Thou shalt not commit adultery.' We didn't know what it meant. But after that we all got into a fight and the nuns had to come and separate us. And then my nun told me that she wasn't very clever either, and she'd given it up herself and trusted that God was right. And if you and your mother and this gentleman don't do the same thing, either you are all as clever as paint or you are all wretched, like I was. So now," said Anisetta, fumbling in her handbag, "I leave it all to Sant' Agata."

She found the medallion and held it by its chain for the Marquis to see.

He took it in his long fingers and examined it closely with his long eyes.

"Who is she?"

"She was a saint who lived in Catania. She was a very good woman so the Romans cut off her breasts. But it didn't get them anywhere, because every time they cut off a breast, God gave her another one."

The Marquis swung the medallion gently to and fro.

"Of course all that isn't true," he said. "But . . ."

"But nothing," Anisetta said sharply. "Of course it *is* true. There is a picture in Catania showing Sant'Agata, and the executioner, and the Roman who is saying 'Cut off her breasts.' And they are all real portraits. Anyone with half an eye can see that merely by looking at it." She took back the medallion abruptly.

"I can quite believe that the executioner really lived," said the Marquis, "and so did the Roman who said 'Cut off her breasts'; because there are always cruel men and people who will carry out their orders. But as far as the saint . . ." and he shrugged his shoulders.

"I think that is the silliest thing I have ever heard," said Anisetta, getting up. "Fancy believing in sinners and not believing in saints."

The Marquis rose, and said humbly:

"I beg your pardon. I did not mean to offend you. I merely wish to learn. Take no notice of what I said. Imagine it was my mother."

"On the first of the month," said Anisetta nodding. "Very well."

But she did not sit down, so the Marquis had to walk beside her.

"Thank you," he said. "Pretending that I'm my mother again, may I say that I don't believe in miracles? Now, what would you answer to that, if you were me and this were the first of the month?"

"I should answer that personally I don't believe that people walk upside-down," said Anisetta. "That's what I would tell your mother."

"Splendid!" said the Marquis. "And I can just see my

mother's face." They walked on for a while, and the Marquis waited for Anisetta to continue. When she did not, he said tentatively:

"But when my mother had recovered from her astonishment, I think she would say that, for her part, she quite agreed with you. People do not walk upside-down. At least, only a very small minority do."

"Your mother would be wrong, which I must say does not surprise me very much. She seems to be wrong about a great number of things."

"I do agree with you," said the Marquis, "that is just how I feel about her myself, especially on the first of the month. But why would she be wrong?"

"People do walk upside-down."

"Where?"

"Surely you can guess!" said Anisetta.

The Marquis shook his head.

"Why in that continent I always forget."

"Australia!" said the Marquis. "So they do!"

Anisetta nodded. "It's the only thing I can ever remember about it and it's so silly I can't believe it. But I'm told it's true. And if God can make millions of people walk upside-down, wicked and good people all alike, I think he'd find it quite easy to give a saint back her breast as a sign and a favor."

"My mother," said the Marquis, "is very shortly going to have the worst ten minutes of her life."

They came to the iron gates of the garden and moved out into the road.

"All the same," said the Marquis, "it does seem easier to believe in sinners rather than saints. I mean," he added hastily, "for people like myself who haven't got your intellectual powers."

"I haven't got any intellectual powers," said Anisetta, a little stiffly. "I'm just an ordinary woman."

"You are an extraordinarily beautiful woman," said the Marquis.

Anisetta smiled. "Well, maybe I have thought one or two things out," she said, mollified.

"You have thought things out from alpha to omega," said the Marquis gallantly. "But that is why I am surprised that you believe in saints. Don't you find this a very wicked world?"

"There's my hotel," said Anisetta, and then:

"Yes. But not as wicked a world as it might be."

"I suppose not. But when you think of the horrible things people do to other people every day, you must admit it's not for want of trying."

"No," said Anisetta, "you misunderstand me." She paused. "I wonder why there are all those policemen on my hotel-steps?" she said, half to herself. And then aloud, she went on:

"The world isn't as wicked a place as it might be, because *I* don't cut off people's breasts, and *I* don't put them in prison and *I* don't make myself a beast. I don't know what you mean by alfa and omigger but I think that's all there's really to be said about right and wrong."

"Madame," said the Marquis, "you have this morning made your first and always your most devoted disciple. I cannot say that I am no longer an Existentialist. I am sure you will understand that it is not yet the first of the month. But I profess myself willing, and eager, to learn my errors." With that he took her hand and kissed it.

Anisetta gave a little scream. She pressed her free hand to her mouth. She opened her dark eyes as wide as they would go, and went white to the lips.

The Marquis straightened up in alarm. He followed her wide-eyed look. He saw the hotel-steps. A man of any other nation would have said:

"What's wrong?"

But the Marquis de Sallotte with generations of history behind him, instantly bowed and said:

"Ah! your husband! Leave it to me."

And smoothly indicating with a gesture an alleyway down which Anisetta could disappear, he made off at an easy pace to the group on the hotel-steps.

*   *   *

Five minutes later Anisetta, looking up the alleyway, saw the Marquis stroll casually past its entrance.

"Hsst," she said.

The Marquis, paused, pretended to search for the alley's name-plate, pretended even more elaborately to check this with an entry in a pocketbook and nodding—theatrically—to himself, made down the alley to Anisetta.

When he reached her he took her arm and drew her into the shelter of a doorway.

"You are safe," he said. "Your husband has been arrested."

"He is not my husband," said Anisetta. "He is my lover. His name is Professor Lissom. I just caught a glimpse of him in between all the policemen."

The Marquis snapped his fingers in irritation.

"Of course he is your lover," he said, "how stupid of me not to guess. That is why he hit the policeman."

"What did he hit the policeman for?"

"He was defending your honor," said the Marquis, with respect.

"Wouldn't he defend my honor if he were my husband?" asked Anisetta, preparing, on her part to defend Aquila.

"Yes," said the Marquis, "but not so precipitately. A married man will of course, in the last resort, lay down his life in defense of his wife's good name. But experience has usually taught him to approach the question in a mellow spirit of reasonableness. Your lover, however, hit the gendarme, according to the concierge who informed me of the cause of the disturbance, before the unfortunate man had said two words."

"What were those two words?" asked Anisetta.

"He said—forgive me—that you were passing clumsily forged money."

"The liar!" said Anisetta.

"The rat," agreed the Marquis.

"The slanderer," stormed Anisetta.

"The assassin!" the Marquis politely concurred.

"Uncle Domenico's never done a clumsy job in his life."

"And should you," continued the Marquis, scarcely hearing Anisetta's last words, "should you give me the word, I would be glad to cram the words down his neck. I would even, provided he is an officer, challenge him to a duel."

Anisetta was looking in her bag. She produced a bundle of notes.

"If the French Government has currency notes half as beautiful as the ones that Uncle Domenico makes," she said indignantly, "then all I can say is that they're very lucky." She riffled through the bundle.

Then she said:

"Ooo!"

She looked closely at a note. Then she said:

"Ooo dear!"

Silently she passed the note across to the Marquis. It was for a large denomination of francs and one half of it was exquisitely engraved. On the other half, however, which was more rough, were pencilled, in Italian, remarks such as 'Scroll poor: improve.' and 'thicker numeral.'

Anisetta said:

"It must have slipped in by mistake."

The Marquis swallowed and said:

"Indeed it must. Where did you get it?"

"From my uncle by marriage, Domenico," she said.

"Where did he get it?"

"He made it."

"But my dear lady, did you know he made it?"

"Of course."

"But you can get into serious trouble," said the Marquis. "In fact you are, if I am not mistaken, already in it."

"Yes," said Anisetta, "if one of those got in the notes I gave to the hall-porter to pay the taxi driver. But the others are bound to be all right. During the war the Allies gave Uncle Domenico a decoration. They said the trouble he caused the Germans was worth two divisions. They said he was a great artist."

"Yes, but this isn't wartime," said the Marquis, but shakily.

"You mean I can't use these?" said Anisetta, showing him a handful of Uncle Domenico's completed final states.

"I certainly do."

Anisetta nodded grimly.

"I see. It's those politicians. Always up to tricks. They never say the same thing two years running. It was the same before the war and it's the same today. . . .' she said.

"I quite agree," said the Marquis hastily, glancing nervously over his shoulder. "But the point is, what are you going to do now?"

Anisetta heaved a sigh.

"It's difficult," she admitted. "I can't go back to Lissom. And I suppose because of all this political wangling, I'm more or less without a penny. Of course, I could write to my husband."

"I don't think that will be necessary," said the Marquis. "The concierge said that your lover has wired him to come immediately."

"He has?" said Anisetta, hope dawning in her eyes.

"Yes," said the Marquis. "If you—" he stopped, and began again. "If you care to hide until this blows over, I have a little apartment . . . nothing very smart I'm afraid, because, as you know, my mother is very tight with my allowance and . . ."

But Anisetta was no longer listening to him. She was clutching her medallion of Sant'Agata, and muttering.

Suddenly her face cleared. She nodded to herself. She turned to the Marquis.

"I should be delighted to hide in your apartment," she said.

The Marquis gasped.

"My darling," he said. "You really mean it?"

"I do," said Anisetta. "Let's go."

"By all means," said the Marquis with enthusiasm, and taking her arm, he led her at a run out of the far end of the alley.

As he peered up and down the road into which the alley led, checking that the way was clear, Anisetta asked him in a fairly casual voice:

"You did say that you would fight a duel for me, didn't you?"

"Yes," said the Marquis, "but it won't be necessary now."

Anisetta smiled. She put her medallion back in her bag.

"You never know," she said.

CHAPTER VIII

DR. ZICHY'S PETARD

"Lissom. *Mad*," said Aquila, sadly. "That great brain; that great engine shaken loose from its . . . its . . ."

"Moorings," suggested Uncle Giorgio.

"You do not moor engines," said Aquila.

There was a short silence.

"That great brain, felled like a forest giant," said Aquila. "It is a great tragedy."

He shook his head and stared through the Le Corbusier window at the boulevard below.

Uncle Giorgio nodded, and vacantly turned the pages of a psycho-analytic review. The only other person in the waiting room, a young man with round spectacles and a close-cropped head, looked keenly from Aquila to Giorgio, but said nothing.

A nurse came in.

"Messieurs," she said, in a very precise voice, "Dr. Zichy will see you in a few minutes. This is unusual. Dr. Zichy does not usually see people without an appointment, and you have given him short notice."

"I apologize to Dr. Zichy," said Aquila. "But my uncle and I arrived in Paris only yesterday morning. We are actually here to find—to see—my wife. But when I read of this terrible tragedy that has happened to Professor Lissom, I immediately rang the sanatorium and they told me to come along."

"*They* told you!" said the nurse with indignation. "*They* have no consideration for Dr. Zichy. I wish *they* would remember that if it were not for Dr. Zichy's *genius* they would be out of a job."

She recovered herself.

"Anyway," she said, "since you're here, Dr. Zichy will see you. It will mean putting off Madame la Duchesse."

Aquila blushed, half with pleasure at being thus even remotely connected with a Duchesse and half with social embarrassment at having inconvenienced her. He had read, with difficulty but also with eager admiration, Marcel Proust. He often felt that if there had been something in his childhood which he had forgotten (like the celebrated cake) he too could one day write a very long book about his innner self. Unfortunately his family was always able to tell him, day by day and almost hour by hour, what had happened to him virtually since his conception. Sicilian families have vivid and frank memories. But at least he now moved on the margins of the Guermantes Way.

"Kindly also convey my profound apologies to Madame la Duchesse," he said, wondering which Duchesse it was or whether, since the war, there was only one left.

"I'll try," said the nurse doubtfully. "But she's a determined woman. The last time Dr. Zichy broke an appointment she went to the Galeries Lafayette and spent a quarter of an hour shop-lifting. It's a thing she's never done before, but as she made clear to Dr. Zichy, she's quite prepared to do it again. However," she said, "I'll do my best."

"Thank you very much indeed," said Aquila fervently, and the nurse left the room, saying:

"I'll tell you when Dr. Zichy is ready for you."

Aquila sat down in a Le Corbusier chair.

"It's really very kind of Zichy to see us," he said to Uncle Giorgio. Giorgio was biting his moustache in an endeavor to follow a case-history in the psycho-analytic magazine which promised to be remarkably interesting, not to say weird.

"Eh?" said Uncle Giorgio.

"I say that it's very kind of Zichy. You may not know it, but since the death of Freud he is the greatest living psychologist. In fact he has even broken away from the teachings of his master and struck out on a line of his own. He says that Freud placed too much stress on sexual matters."

Giorgio glanced at his magazine.

"Oh well, I don't know," he said, "one has to face the facts of human nature, however extraordinary they may be."

With that he returned to the facts of life as faced by a young lady curtly described in the article as Miss B.

Aquila was a little annoyed to find someone reading while he was talking. He could not remember that it had ever happened before.

"I'm afraid you find that journal a little beyond you," he said with a tolerant smile, hoping that, as usual, he would be asked to explain.

"Yes," said Uncle Giorgio, "but it is remarkable how quickly I am learning." He wetted his finger and turning the page, eagerly resumed his study.

"Dr. Zichy," said Aquila, rather more loudly than was necessary, "believes that most of our mental troubles are due to the fact that we fall out of harmony with other human beings. It is as though we were singing in a choir and we suddenly found ourselves singing flat and not being able to stop."

Half hearing this Uncle Giorgio murmured:

"Yes. Miss B. certainly wasn't able to stop, was she? But I don't really think she wanted to. Not when she'd got well set," he added, and wetting his finger, turned another page.

"As that magazine no doubt fully explains," said Aquila with a touch of sarcasm, "Dr. Zichy's system is to persuade his patients of the beauty, so to speak, of the tune which the rest of the choir is singing and how ugly it is to sing flat. He can be said to have given psycho-analysis a spiritual elevation which it badly needed."

"Yes," said Uncle Giorgio. He put down the magazine and mopping his moustache, said "It certainly did."

"You misunderstand me," said Aquila.

Uncle Giorgio pulled himself together.

"How stupid of me," he said. "Please explain again."

This, of course, Aquila was very willing to do. But he did not get the chance.

"He means that Dr. Zichy is a genius and a genius in his own right. I quite agree with him."

The person who said this was the young man with cropped hair and glasses.

He turned his head like a scientific instrument being brought smoothly to bear on Uncle Giorgio, and said what he had to say with overwhelming decision. Besides, he said it in Neapolitan.

Sicily is separated from Italy by a stretch of water only four miles wide. But Sicilians refer, pityingly, to all the other Italians as Continentals. If you were to tell a Sicilian that certain of the people of, say Trentino, had begun to eat their fathers, he would not be suprised. He would merely wonder why he had not seen it in *La Corriere di Sicilia*. Trentino is a long way north. If you said the same things about the people of Naples he would still not be surprised (neither would the Neapolitans—they are a full-blooded lot), but he would feel a little sorry for the eaten fathers. Naples is getting on for being in the South, the only part of Italy which counts. Besides, the Neapolitans speak Italian with a strong accent, and so do the Sicilians.

Aquila, Giorgio and the young man with the cropped hair therefore immediately all shook hands.

His name was Chichu Bambara. He was 27. He was the son of that famous Bambara whose name, supported by smiling cupids, appears on every bottle of a certain Neapolitan wine.

"Yes," said Bambara, in his remarkably sure tones, "you can take it from me that Dr. Zichy is a very great man. You may be certain that your friend is in safe hands. Look at *me*!"

It was of course, a manner of speaking: but Bambara made it sound like the command of an overbearing snake to a recalcitrant rabbit. Uncle Giorgio and Aquila looked, as they were ordered, into the gleaming circles of his glasses.

"You won't believe it, but once I was as mad as a hatter," he said.

Uncle Giorgio shivered.

"Really?" he said. "Surely no."

"Surely *yes*." said the young man. "Before I was twenty I hated everybody. I would not play football. I would not go to parties. I was anti-social, secretive, individualistic and rebellious to authority. I used to lock myself in my bedroom and write poetry."

"Yes, but . . ." Aquila protested.

Bambara moved his scientific instrument until it was precisely adjusted upon Aquila.

"Poetry of no social significance whatsoever."

"Ah!" said Aquila. "Oh! I see: Tsk! Tsk!"

"Fortunately my father is a prosperous bourgeois and could afford to send me abroad for treatment. He sent me to Dr. Zichy. Dr. Zichy conditioned me to see myself as a member of the community with duties towards other people. He showed me that to be out of step was to be walking in one's sleep. He taught me to value the warm companionship of my fellow men, to be loyal to them, to put other people before myself and to lay down my life, if needs be, for the sake of my comrades."

"Brava!" said Aquila. "Bravissima!"

"Finely put," said Giorgio. "Very finely put."

"I have a copy here," said Bambara, and instantly produced a neatly written sheet of paper containing a poem in free verse.

Giorgio took it.

"Read it," said Bambara, and composed himself until this should be done.

When Giorgio had finished, Bambara said:

"What do you think of it?"

Giorgio hesitated.

"It is wonderful," said Bambara, with the decision of a reviewer hailing his mistress's latest novel.

"It certainly is not in the least morbid," agreed Giorgio. But Bambara clearly did not regard this as enough.

"It should do very well in America," said Giorgio.

"Yes. *When the time comes,*" said Bambara, with a menacing nod.

A little silence fell upon the waiting room. Aquila, piqued at not having his opinion asked on the poem, said peevishly:

"But—excuse my asking—if you've been cured so wonderfully by Dr. Zichy, why are you waiting here?"

"I want to see him."

"Obviously," said Aquila. "But do you want to see him in his professional capacity?"

"I want to see him in his capacity as an enemy of the working class," said Bambara, promptly and clearly.

The next moment Aquila and Giorgio both leapt to their feet. Bambara, with a neatness which won Giorgio's admiration, had produced a small automatic.

*   *   *

Bambara nodded his head towards Dr. Zichy's consulting room door and very slightly waved the gun.

"I am going to shoot him," he said with great simplicity, and with another neat gesture, put the gun back in his pocket.

"Put that gun away!" said Aquila.

Uncle Giorgio pointed out reasonably that Bambara had already done so.

"Yes," said Aquila, "but I couldn't get my breath back to say it before," and then slipping into the broadest and, even to Neapolitans, the most incomprehensible Sicilian dialect he said:

"Anyway, don't stand there making obvious remarks. Do something."

The young man, finding that he could not follow what they were saying, lost interest. He began studying Dr. Zichy's door as though, with sufficient effort and time, he would be able to see through it.

"I don't quite see what I can do," continued Uncle Giorgio, still in Sicilian.

"Draw your gun," said Aquila.

"My gun," said Uncle Giorgio, "is in your pocket, if you remember." And seeing Aquila move his hand he immediately continued, "A fact which is somewhat fortunate because if there is one man in the world who is a fraction quicker on the draw than I am it is our friend Chichu Bambara."

The young man, hearing his name mentioned, brought his attention sharply back to Giorgio and Aquila.

Aquila jumped a little.

"If we can't shoot him we must try reason," he said rapidly to Uncle Giorgio out of the corner of his mouth.

Uncle Giorgio approved of this. After twenty years of study of banditry, both practical (on the mountain tops) and theoretic (from international politics as gleaned from newspapers), Uncle Giorgio had made up his mind that there were only two things which anyone ever says in a crisis. One is, 'If we can't shoot him, we must try reason.' The other is 'If he won't listen to reason, he must be shot.' The first is for persons, Ministers of War, nations and alliances which are in an inferior position vis à vis the enemy. The second is for persons, Ministers of War, nations and alliances in a superior position vis à vis the enemy. Thus it will be seen that Giorgio was no pessimist. He believed that reason has a definite place in human affairs. That is why he approved of Aquila's statement.

On the other hand, it did not seem that Chichu Bambara approved of Aquila at all.

He took out his gun again, smoothly slipped back the safety-catch and as smoothly said:

"I do not like you talking out of the corner of your mouth and I do hope you are not planning any tricks because I should have no hesitation in shooting you: although, perhaps, I should have regrets, since you are a fellow-countryman. You also appear to be intelligent. Since you are intelligent you will not need to be told that what I have just said is the truth. If I were not prepared to shoot you I would not have told you that I am going to shoot Dr. Zichy."

"But," said Aquila, and then said "But" again, and in a

more manly register, "whyever do you want to shoot Dr. Zichy?"

"A fair question," said the young man, "and one that I hoped you would ask. I would like an independent witness to my motives." He put his free hand into his jacket pocket. Aquila closed his eyes.

"You may open your eyes," said Bambara, after a moment. "It is only a newspaper."

He held it out to Aquila.

Aquila, with some hesitation took it. It was folded so as to show an article. The article was headed by a photograph of Dr. Zichy.

"Well," said Bambara, "don't you see now why I have got to shoot him?"

"No," said Aquila. "Why?"

"He does not believe in the inheritance of acquired characteristics," said Bambara with an expression of great discust. "You would scarcely believe it of a man of his distinction, but nobody is above a bribe."

"No," said Uncle Giorgio.

"I'm glad you agree with me," said Bambara.

"In a general sense, I do," said Uncle Giorgio. "But what is the inheritance of acquired characteristics?"

"It refers to characteristics which are first acquired and are then believed by every honest scientist with a sense of social responsibilities and a proper grasp of the antinomies contained in the world political situation, to be inherited. Certain reptilian lackeys of big business say they are not."

"I can just see them," said Uncle Giorgio.

"Are you a party member too?" asked Bambara with a flash of boyish eagerness.

"No," said Uncle Giorgio. "I meant that I can see the reptilian lackeys. They are sitting up on the box of a pumpkin coach drawn by mice."

Bambara's face became expressionless.

"I do not follow you," he said.

He rose firmly to his feet and pointed his gun full at Uncle Giorgio.

With a great wave of relief, Aquila heard high-pitched voices from outside the room, and the noise of the door opening behind him.

He had prepared a phrase in his mind—'That man is mad; seize him: he is armed!'—and he turned to deliver it.

He was almost trampled underfoot by the nurse, who, walking backwards, was speaking volubly to an elderly woman. The elderly woman—clearly the Duchesse—moved with such state and circumstance that she might well have rolled in on four wheels, surrounded by outriders.

As they moved across the room Aquila could gather that the Duchesse was inexorably bent upon keeping her appointment, while the nurse was bent on keeping Dr. Zichy's most valuable client, and that she was perjuring her soul to do it.

Aquila also gathered that Bambara had his gun pointed at him, but through his pocket.

Aquila opened his mouth to speak.

Giorgio shook his head.

Aquila closed his mouth.

The nurse pushed open the door of Dr. Zichy's room with her haunch, both her hands being busy, in aid of her tongue, in apologizing to the Duchesse.

They disappeared and the door closed on affable bellowings that Aquila presumed came from Dr. Zichy, unconscious of the danger in which he stood.

Aquila stole a glance at Bambara's pocket, and Bambara, with a look that for him was almost playful, waggled his gun at him.

Aquila remembered that people threatened by armed madmen always played for time. But he soon saw that this thought was not helpful. Aquila had plenty of time. The trouble was that he had no idea what to do with it.

In desperation he turned to look at Uncle Giorgio. He found Giorgio turning the pages of his magazine.

"Really, Uncle Giorgio," burst out Aquila, "this is no time to catch up on your reading."

"I've never known a time when it was more urgent," said Uncle Giorgio, rapidly licking over the pages of the psycho-analytic magazine. "I happened to notice an article in here by the man who has so annoyed Chichu Bambara. Now if I can understand what Dr. Zichy's teaching is I might be able to persuade our friend to spare his life. . . . Ah! here it is," he said and flattened the magazine on his knee.

Aquila, peering, saw that it was headed:

BEYOND THE GOD-CONCEPT : A PSYCHIATRIST'S FAITH

"Or," continued Uncle Giorgio, running his eye over the heading, "on the other hand I may consider it wiser not to interfere."

He at once began to read the article with great absorption.

"I can save you the trouble of reading that article," said Bambara. "Dr. Zichy is a great scientist. Every word of what he says is true, with the exception of what he says about the inheritance of acquired characteristics for the sake of Wall Street dollars. I am not going to shoot him because he is a bad psychologist: I am going to shoot him because he is an exceedingly good one. And," he added catching Aquila's eye, "I think I am going to shoot *you,* not because you are not a very likable fellow, but because you cannot resist a desire to interrupt."

Once more Aquila closed his mouth, and this time firmly.

"As I was saying," Bambara went on, "Dr. Zichy taught me to be loyal and comradely instead of a lone-wolf. He taught me to be socially adjusted instead of running against the stream. Above all, he taught me to put other people before myself. Very well. I joined the Party. The Party believes that acquired characteristics are inherited. It believes that people who say that they are not, are dogs, jackals, imperialist hyenas and anti-social. I have sent Dr. Zichy several anonymous warnings and even a pamphlet. He has no excuse; and for that matter, neither would I have if I failed to do my loyal and selfless duty by the Party. The Party does not actually order me to kill him, but they do not have to, because thanks to Dr. Zichy I am socially adjusted and mentally in step. I am sorry that Dr. Zichy has become himself anti-social, but since he has, I must kill him."

Bambara moved his spectacles round until they blazed precisely upon Dr. Zichy's door. Already mesmerized by Bambara's even voice and the smooth flow of his argument, Aquila too looked at the door.

It opened. Dr. Zichy walked briskly through it.

Bambara suddenly stiffened.

Aquila screamed, "No. No. Don't do it!" and clapped his hands to his ears.

Uncle Giorgio finished the article and closed the magazine. He said, "I must confess, I really don't know what to say," and seeing Dr. Zichy, politely arose.

Dr. Zichy clicked his tongue against his teeth.

"How very nervous we are today!" he exclaimed.

*   *   *

He was a very tall Hungarian with tightly curling hair, that was a little grey, a snub nose and a boyish face. Happiness (to use the words of many of his women patients) streamed from every feature.

He walked buoyantly across the waiting room, and taking hold of Aquila's hands (which, it will be remembered, were clapped against his ears) Zichy gently brought them away and downwards, so that he stood holding them and gazing magnetically into Aquila's eyes.

"There," he said richly, "that's better. We are calm now. You are Professor Lissom's friend, is it not so? Yes, it is so. And you were afraid that I was going to give you bad news. Is that not so? But it is not so. I am not going to give you bad news, and now we are calm." His voice grew even richer and he emphasized his points by gently pumphandling Aquila's arm. "It is so stupid of us, but it is the thing which we do not know that makes us afraid. Yet is it not stupid to be afraid of the thing we do not know? We must not be as savages trembling in the dark, must we?"

"No," answered Aquila. Indeed, that is what everybody always answered.

"Good," said Dr. Zichy, "already the cure begins."

And this is what Zichy always said. It had brought him a fortune.

"Never," he repeated, to give good measure, "be afraid of what you do not know." He poured happiness round the room for a moment, exuding it, so to speak, from the interstices of his faultless teeth.

"I remember your face," he said to Bambara, catching sight of him. But as Dr. Zichy was speaking in English of which Bambara knew very little, the gunman did not change his expression in the slightest.

"He is an old patient of yours," said Aquila with the most significant of looks.

"And I can see that you are already impressed by the calm way he faces the world. He is quite an object lesson to you, young man, if I may say so," said Zichy, while Aquila reflected that Zichy was the sort of man who would say anything he pleased, with or without permission, for there was no way of stopping the boisterous torrent of his talk. "I remember you quite well," said Zichy, swivelling his eupeptic charm upon the boy. "Your name is Bambara."

Bambara rose, his hand still in his pocket. Aquila clenched his teeth till his jaw ached. But Bambara merely bowed.

"And this is Mr. Morales, my uncle," said Aquila jerkily, to get Dr. Zichy out of what he presumed to be the line of fire.

Zichy shook hands.

"Now," he said, "I want you to share with me in solving a little human problem. You are anxious to know about Professor Lissom, is that not so? It is so. And I am anxious to tell you everything, but everything. So. But in my consulting room there is a lady who insists upon seeing me. She says she will have a crisis of the nerves if I do not see her immediately. Now what are we to do?"

He ruffled his greying curls, imitating great perplexity.

Bambara, standing behind him, slightly raised the pocket in which he had his gun.

"What shall we do, eh?" said Aquila in a falsetto.

"Please, please, there is no need to excite yourself," said Dr. Zichy to him. "These little things can all be smoothed out if we get together. So. We get together. I will tell you in three little words about your friend, and then you will go away. You will leave me your address and I will telephone you. Is that not so? It is so. Now Professor Lissom is as you know a philosopher."

"Really?" said Aquila with hysterical brightness. "How interesting! How fascinating! *How* fascinating! Do let us SIT DOWN and you can tell me all about it."

Zichy ignored this, but Aquila had little time to notice it. He was absorbed in the fact that Bambara, disturbed by Aquila's tone, had moved his gun so that it covered him.

"Professor Lissom's great work as a young man was in the metaphysical foundations of causality," said Zichy. "I will explain. Suppose that you hit one billiard ball against two others. This will make what is called a cannon. Is that not so?"

"It is so," said Uncle Giorgio.

"Very well. If you knew everything about the billiard balls and everything about the force of your stroke, you would know exactly what was going to happen to all three balls."

"It's the same with *bullets*," said Aquila, pointing with his eyebrows.

"Yes, no doubt, but we are not talking about bullets. We are talking about Professor Lissom," said Zichy with a certain amount of irritation. "And Professor Lissom, I am sorry to say, no longer believes that we can know everything about the billiard balls and so predict what will happen to them. In fact he no longer believes in Cause and Effect at all."

"That is stupid," said Aquila quickly. "If somebody for instance were to fire a bullet into your back now because of some fancied grudge, you would fall dead," he said. But he was careful to say all this in a very even tone of voice and with his most colloquial English pronunciation.

Zichy regarded him curiously. To do this he had to turn slightly. Bambara shifted so as to remain directly behind him.

"Do you often," asked Zichy, "dream about dead people? Corpses, for instance, and murders? Forgive me for asking, but it may be a clue to your condition."

"No," said Aquila miserably, "but I have a feeling that I'm going to have some pretty bad dreams about them in the future."

"So. There you go again—worrying about what you don't know," said Zichy.

"On the contrary, I am worrying about what *you* do not know," said Aquila, but with a shade too much spirit. At Bambara's unspoken invitation, he fell silent.

"To return to your distinguished friend," Zichy swept on. "He is suffering, at the moment, from a temporary maladjustment. He no longer believes that the Universe is governed by law. He is wedded to what I might call the Uncertainty Principle. I will explain the Uncertainty Principle in three words."

"I can explain it in one," said Uncle Giorgio. "Dogs."

Dr. Zichy was dumfounded.

"*So,*" he said, "My nurse must have been talking."

"I have been doing no such thing," said a woman's voice, and they turned to find the nurse standing in the door. "But the Duchesse is talking quite a lot, especially about shop-lifting."

"Excuse me," said Dr. Zichy hastily, turning back to Aquila and Giorgio. "I must go."

"You must!" said Aquila.

"But you will not fail to leave me your address," said Zichy with a telling look at Aquila. "I may possibly be of help not only to your friend."

"You'll find us . . ." began Aquila.

"At the apartment of the Marquis de Sallotte, 14 Villa Seurat," finished Giorgio, checking his information from a postcard which he took from his pocket.

"Where?" asked Aquila, bewildered.

"Never mind," said Uncle Giorgio. "That is where we shall be."

Dr. Zichy said, in reverent tones:

"Did you say the Marquis de Sallotte?"

"I did," said Uncle Giorgio.

"A friend of yours?"

"A friend of the family's," agreed Uncle Giorgio.

"My dear sir," said Zichy, ruffling his curls, "how can I ever apologize to you for keeping you waiting here?"

Bambara's hand began to move slowly from his pocket.

"This is no time for fine manners," said Aquila, but Uncle Giorgio, after a glance at Bambara and a last glance at his psychological magazine, began to move towards the door.

Zichy, bowing, accompanied them.

At the door, Uncle Giorgio said:

"Pray do not come any further. We must not take up any more of your time. After all, you have so little of it."

He firmly shut the door on Zichy and Bambara, and as firmly took Aquila's arm and led him down the stairs to the exit.

CHAPTER IX

DUEL IN MONTPARNASSE

They stood outside the house in the road in Montparnasse
called the Villa Seurat. Aquila barely gave the house, or even
Montparnasse, a glance. Half an hour before Aquila would
have found his being in so famed a place as Montparnasse
the apex of intellectual pleasure. But now:

"I'm sure I heard a bang," was all that he said.

"It was the door slamming," said Uncle Giorgio.

"It was after the door slammed, just as we were on our way
down the stairs. And it wasn't a slam, it was a bang."

This was not the first time Aquila had said this. He had
repeated it with deepening shades of moral anxiety all the way
across Paris in the taxi.

"If Bambara let off his gun in that small room," said
Uncle Giorgio soothingly, "it wouldn't sound like a bang. It
would sound like the roof giving way."

"I think you are making that up and relying on your reputation with firearms to make me believe it," said Aquila cen-
soriously. "You know very well that we ought never to have left
Dr. Zichy. How can I ever square my conscience with the fact
that we have deserted a fellow human being in danger of
his life?"

"I'll tell you," said Uncle Giorgio. "Meanwhile, let us
cross the road."

Once on the other side of the road, Uncle Giorgio began
searching the front of the house outside of which they had
been standing. With a preoccupied air, he began:

"In the first place Dr. Zichy is scarcely a fellow human
being."

"This is no time for sophistries," said Aquila.

"He is much more," said Giorgio, ignoring him but still paying great attention to the front of the house. "He is Dr. Zichy."

"Probably by now the late Dr. Zichy," said Aquila, flagellating his conscience.

"Now, Dr. Zichy does not believe in right and wrong," Uncle Giorgio went on, "as I discovered to my great interest by reading his article. He believes that human beings are fallible—oh, *very* fallible—but does not believe that they should be unduly worried when they do wrong. They should not for instance ask pardon of what Dr. Zichy calls the God-concept. Dr. Zichy does not find it necessary to believe in God. Not at least since he set up his own practice. No. The only sin that Dr. Zichy reluctantly admits in a wrong-doer is not immediately consulting Dr. Zichy. In fact Dr. Zichy says the sin is really ignorance."

"So did Socrates," said Aquila impatiently. "But where does that get you?"

It got Uncle Giorgio, surprisingly, into the opening phrase of the 'Letter Song' from Massenet's "Werther," which he sang in a loud Italian tenor.

Aquila blushed, and glanced ashamedly at a passer-by who was staring curiously.

"I do not think you should indulge in that Sicilian habit of singing on the slightest provocation," he said in an undertone to Uncle Giorgio, "especially when you are in a foreign country. It is one of the things that get us a reputation for being flippant."

"There is nothing flippant about my singing," said Uncle Giorgio, "not when I sing really loud. It is like the giraffe's neck: it strikes one with awe at the strangeness of creation."

He went on to demonstrate this fully in the next three phrases of the song.

"I can't see anything wrong in Dr. Zichy's theory," said Aquila, with the elaborate unconcern of a parent whose small child has just committed a heinous social blunder. "Surely the wise thing to do *is* to tell Dr. Zichy. I only wish that I'd told him he was going to be shot."

Uncle Giorgio broke off in the middle of the aria. "That is the point," he said. "You couldn't. Because if you had you would have been shot yourself. Therefore a unique occasion arose where someone could not tell Dr. Zichy. Therefore," finished Uncle Giorgio triumphantly, "you could do no wrong."

Aquila snorted. "It is a pity that you chose to be a bandit. You had a wonderful career before you in the Church," he said. "You would have been an enormous success in the confessional."

"Da, da, da DAR da di," resumed Uncle Giorgio, singing happily at the house opposite.

He finished the aria. Then, when he had got back a little of his breath he said:

"Talking of priests, there is the woman that Father Pipo married you to not so very long ago."

"Whom do you mean?" said Aquila.

"I mean Anisetta," said Giorgio.

"What!" shouted Aquila, "where?"

"Standing at the window," said Uncle Giorgio pointing to the opposite house, "blowing kisses at you like a lunatic."

And so she was.

*   *   *

St. Paul gave very strict instructions to the early Christians that they should bridle their tongues. When the Italians were converted, Providence, relenting, gave them the gift of talking with their hands. The Sicilians, as is proper with gifts from Providence, put it to its fullest use.

Thus, Anisetta, standing behind a tall window such as is found in painters' studios, now said by gestures to Giorgio and her husband:

"I am very glad to see you and I do love my husband but where have you been all this time never mind you are here no DON'T come up. There is somebody behind me in the room but if you wait a minute I shall come downstairs and meet you in the street and I do love my husband but he is a very wicked boy."

Anisetta disappeared. Aquila turned to Uncle Giorgio and said:

"But this is amazing. How in the name of heaven did you trace her?"

"Oh, it was really nothing," said Uncle Giorgio modestly.

"Nothing! It's practically a miracle," said Aquila glowing with an admiration such as he had never before shown for his uncle. "It's a piece of detective work worthy of Sherlock Holmes."

"Of course," admitted Uncle Giorgio, "it did involve a certain amount of deduction."

"But the clues! How did you find those? And you so quiet about it all the time."

"Naturally," said Uncle Giorgio, "one relies on a certain amount of luck in the matter of clues."

"Luck!" said Aquila. "All great men describe their discoveries as luck. You may call it luck that Sir Alexander Fleming picked up the particular piece of glass on which penicillin was growing, but it was Sir Alexander Fleming who picked it up."

"If you put it like that," said Uncle Giorgio, fingering his moustache, and with something of a blush.

"It's knowing how to use the clues that luck has put in your way that makes genius," said Aquila sagely.

"There," said Uncle Giorgio, waving to Anisetta as she emerged from the doorway, "I agree with you."

"From now on," said Aquila, watching Anisetta cross the road, "you will have my profoundest respect."

Anisetta, coming first to Uncle Giorgio, flung her arms round his neck, kissed him and said:

"I'm so glad you got my postcard. I wondered if it would be delivered because I had to post it without a stamp."

Then she put her arms round her husband's neck and kissed him. But as a gesture it was spoiled by Aquila's spluttering:

"Uncle! Of all the shameful tricks!"

When he had disentangled himself from Anisetta's arms, after briefly looking delighted to see her, Aquila said to his uncle:

"Why didn't you tell me Anisetta had sent a postcard?"

"Because he has got common sense which is a great deal more than I can say for you," said Anisetta. "If he'd shown you the postcard you would have spent the next ten weeks wrestling with your conscience as to whether it would be progressive to come and take your wife away from another man."

"I did think something like that," admitted Giorgio. "But *are* you living with another man?"

"Yes," said Anisetta, with more satisfaction than Aquila quite liked.

"But Lissom, poor man," said Giorgio, "is in a sanatorium. I was very puzzled when I heard it, particularly since the address you gave wasn't Lissom's hotel—or rather, his sanatorium. So I came along hoping to find out."

"And so you shall," said Anisetta. "Come with me." And linking her arms in theirs she led them across the road.

They went into the hallway, and Anisetta stopped beside the concierge's box.

She drew their attention to a board with four little brass frames, in three of which were visiting cards.

"That is the man I am living with," said Anisetta in the calmest of voices, and she pointed to the first card. Giorgio and Aquila read:

LE MARQUIS DE SALLOTTE

"A marquis!" said Aquila. His emotions were mixed. Few men have known what to think on discovering that their wives are loved by socially prominent persons. A man must of course be devoted to his wife but there is a great future in being well-connected: and after all, a man must think of his children.

But Aquila's thoughts were cut short. Anisetta, pointing to the second card, said:

"And that is my lover, too."

With great surprise, Giorgio and Aquila read the second card:

LUCIUS H. LOPER

"Are you living with two men at the same time?" asked Aquila.

"No," said Anisetta. "I am living with three. This one is the third," and she pointed to the last card, which read:

ELLIS PETERS

"Lucius and Ellis," said Anisetta, "are Americans. The Marquis, of course, is French."

Aquila's jaw dropped.

"Well," said Anisetta, "what have you to say?"

But Aquila had nothing to say. He was dumfounded.

"And you, Uncle?"

Giorgio pulled at his moustache for the space of fifteen seconds. Then he answered her question:

"Say, my dear? I should say that to be the mistress of one Frenchman would be natural. To be the mistress of three Frenchmen might be put down to high spirits. But to be the mistress of one Frenchman and two Americans shows a cold-blooded sense of planning, especially in the case of the Americans. I think you owe us an explanation."

"I do," said Anisetta. "And I shall be very happy to make it. But not here. Come into the garden."

She led them through the house into a very pretty courtyard. The house lay on all four sides of a square, stone-flagged space in which were shrubs growing in pots, small stone boxes of flowers and a great old vine. Over all the courtyard was spread a netting made of wire which not only held up the branches of the vine, but caught rubbish which was thrown out of the surrounding windows. In the middle of the courtyard was an iron table with a marble top, and a few chairs. On the table stood a bottle and several glasses.

Anisetta, with much composure, asked Aquila to sit down, which he did with no composure at all. Uncle Giorgio she asked to pour out some of the wine that was in the bottle, and when this was done and he was seated she began.

* * *

"My first lover, the Marquis," she said, "lives in the part of the building which is in front of us. The bedroom is the one with yellow curtains, and instead of calling him the Marquis, in future I shall call him Joel. My second lover, Lucius, lives in the wing on our left. The bedroom had no curtain at all, because he is a very idealistic young man and cannot bring his mind to think of such things as furnishings. I shall call him Lucius because that is his name and he looks just what you would expect a young American called Lucius to look like. My third lover, Ellis, lives in the wing on our right. I do not know which is the bedroom because I have never been into it, since he says it is sacred to his dead wife. However, the drawing room, which is very comfortably furnished, is the one with the velvet hangings that you can just see through the vine leaves. I shall call my third lover Popsy, which is American for father; not a real father but one that they call a sugar-daddy, a word which I can never pronounce properly. So I call him Popsy. Popsy is fifty-seven, Lucius is twenty-three and the Marquis is neither too young nor too old, but just right. I love all three of them and all three of them love me, and I am very happy. What I have just said I have written out on a piece of paper and learned off by heart. If you want to know anything more you must ask me questions."

She finished, and with much newly-found elegance, sipped her wine, glancing at Aquila over the rim of her glass, with an expression which would have suggested to a calmer observer that she was drinking wine to hide a smile.

On the other hand it was plain that Aquila drank his wine to steady his nerves. When he had poured down a whole glassful, he said, as one who must know the worst:

"What about the fourth apartment," and he pointed to the wing of the building that lay behind them.

"At the moment that is empty," said Anisetta. "The concierge has shown me over it. It could be made to look very nice but it will cost a good deal to furnish. The concierge suggests that when I have made my nest-eggs from my three lovers, I should rent it and live in it, so that I can have some privacy, if and when I want it."

"He seems a sensible and experienced man," said Uncle Giorgio. "But what you promised was an explanation."

"Yes," said Aquila, with a hint of truculence. "You promised an explanation. All you have given us so far is a lay-out of the building and short descriptions of the tenants. We don't want to know where you go for your—your affairs—we want to know *why* you go."

"I shall tell you," said Anisetta. "In the first place I have been thinking."

Aquila said suspiciously:

"At any other time I would have said 'Brava.' Now I am not so sure. What have you been thinking about?"

"Right and wrong."

"Principally, I take it, the latter," murmured Uncle Giorgio, glancing at the bedroom windows.

"I daresay I am not very good at it," said Anisetta. "But I have the best of excuses."

"I am glad we are getting to the excuses," said Aquila. "They do seem a little overdue. I hope they are reasonable."

"I am almost bursting with reason," answered Anisetta, "and what is more I have hit upon the most wonderful discovery. At least, Popsy thought of it first, but it was I who put it into practice."

"On the face of it," said Aquila stiffly, "I don't think I shall approve of anything discovered by a man who lets himself be called Popsy. However, I am always open to new ideas. What is it?"

Anisetta took a deep breath:

"Name me one famous person who thought about morals," she said.

"Socrates," Aquila answered.

Anisetta said:

"Socrates was a man?"

"That," said Aquila condescendingly, "may be taken as one of the more firmly established truths. In fact, you can find it where I imagine Popsy found it: namely in any book of Logic. And I suppose you are going to say that since Socrates was a man and all men are mortal, then Socrates was mortal. This is known as the syllogism, which was discovered by Aristotle. And Popsy."

"I am not going to talk any such rigmarole," said Anisetta impatiently. "What I was going to say was that if Socrates was a man then Socrates was not a woman."

Aquila regarded her for a moment in silence.

"Is that your discovery?" he asked.

"Yes," said Anisetta with energy. "It certainly is. And I don't care if Arrisbottle did discover the syllabism; he didn't discover *that*."

"Totle," said Aquila. "Not bottle."

"You know what I meant," said Anisetta, but a little dashed.

Giorgio came to her rescue.

"Of course we know what you meant," he said, "and Aquila is becoming a bit of a pedant. Go on with your discovery."

"Well, then," said Anisetta, thus encouraged, "name me another moralist."

"Plato," said Uncle Giorgio.

"Man or woman?" asked Anisetta.

"Man."

"Right," said Anisetta, "name me another."

"Spinoza," said Aquila.

"Man or woman?" asked Anisetta.

"Man."

"Now another."

"Immanuel Kant."

"Man or woman?"

"Whoever heard of a woman being called Immanuel?" asked Aquila in return.

"Nobody," agreed Anisetta. "And whoever heard of a woman philosopher?"

"Eh?" said Aquila.

Anisetta said, patiently:

"Whoever heard of a woman philosopher? The answer is 'Nobody' because there have never been any. That is the discovery."

There was a long silence between them.

"Well, I'm damned," said Giorgio at length. "Neither have there."

"But there is one now," said Anisetta. "Me."

"That is impossible," said Aquila. "You have never so much as opened a book of moral philosophy in your life."

"So much the better," Anisetta confidently replied. "Popsy says that the first thing that every philosopher does is to prove that every other philosopher is either a fool or a liar. Then somebody comes along and proves that *he* is a fool and a liar, so what is the point of reading their books? Popsy says that there are only two professions in the world where you have to knock down everybody else to get to the top; one is philosophy and the other is prize-fighting. Popsy used to study philosophy but now he is a boxing fan. He says boxing is a cleaner sport because the boxers don't make up their own rules as they go along. Anyway I don't have to knock anyone down because I am the first woman philosopher."

"And what," said Aquila sarcastically, "is your philosophy?"

"Just a minute," she said, "and I will tell you."

She put her hand into the front of her dress and after a moment, produced a crumpled piece of paper. She studied this briefly, and then said:

"I am a Female Hedonist."

"Have you the least idea what Hedonism means?" asked Aquila.

"I have," said Anisetta. "Popsy told me. It means that you say what you want and you make a grab for it, Devil take the hindmost."

"It means, with all due deference to Popsy," said Aquila, "that man seeks his proper end and his proper end is that which gives him the greatest pleasure. But this should not be crudely interpreted to mean that man seeks some crude physical satisfaction. A man may very well desire Honor, Glory or Renown. . . ."

"Or the top brick off the chimney for all I care," said Anisetta. "I am not talking about Man, I am talking about Woman. That is why I call myself a Female. . . ." She consulted the paper. ". . . Hedonist," she said. "And what a woman wants is not Honor or Fame or Glory but a French marquis who is devoted to her, a handsome young American who will make passionate love to her, and a nice, wise old Popsy who will pay all the bills. And I've got 'em all," she said, waving her glass at the three sides of the courtyard in turn.

She then held the glass in front of Giorgio, asked him to fill it, and when this was done, tossed off the wine with a gesture which she had seen in the first act of La Traviata at a performance in Catania.

She laughed gaily.

"And," she said, "I am very, very happy."

*   *   *

When she had repeated all this information several times at the request of Uncle Giorgio, and when at last Aquila fully understood it, Aquila began to grow very sad.

"A woman philosopher!" he said shaking his head. "That is something I never reckoned with." Then after a pause he said quietly to his wife:

"Are you quite sure you are happy?"

"Quite sure," said Anisetta, not at all quietly, but with a voice like a brass gong.

Aquila looked at his boots for a long moment.

"Yes," he said, with a little sigh of resignation. "Yes, of course you would be. Reason is a wonderful thing." He paused. He looked up. "Uncle," he went on, "you might pour me out another glass of wine."

Giorgio did so, and Aquila drank it off at one gulp.

"Anisetta," he said, and a trace of the maudlin appeared in his voice. "Anisetta, are they kind to you, in their various ways?"

"They are kind to me, in their various ways," said Anisetta, firmly.

Aquila said:

"Oh, good."

He paused. Then he said:

"Uncle, you might give me just one more glass of that very good wine."

Giorgio, but this time with some hesitation, did so.

"Thank you," said Aquila and once again he swallowed all the wine in one tilt of the glass. He turned to Anisetta.

"So you're ver' happy," he said. "Ver' happy. Then if you're ver' happy, I'm ver' happy. Splendid! Bravissimo!" He wrinkled up his forehead in a woebegone manner.

"Bravissimo," he repeated, but with extreme dejection.

"It's nice to know you take it so well," said Anisetta, but in a rather anxious voice.

Aquila said:

"Me? Finest thing I ever heard. Three lovers. One husband. One silly li'l fool of a husband."

He shook his head slowly at Giorgio.

"Uncle," he said reproachfully. "Why are you so mean with Popsy's drink? Gimme some more."

He thrust out his glass, insisted that it be fillled, and putting it to his lips, immediately emptied it for the third time. He wiped his lips.

"Nisetta," he said.

"Yes, Aquila," she answered.

"D'you remember our wedding?"

"Of course I do."

"It was ver' nice," he said. Then he added apologetically. "Ver' nice, that is, for simple Sicilians. Six bridesmaids."

Anisetta said: "Four."

"No," argued Aquila, "Six. Counted 'em."

"Then you must have been drinking too much," said Anisetta, taking his glass away from him.

"There were six," he insisted. "Little Caterina. And Rosa. And . . . *How* many did you say?"

Anisetta said: "Four."

Aquila threw up his hands in resignation.

"Then four is right," he said. "You can't be wrong. First Woman Philosopher can't be wrong. No."

He leaned forward over the table and pointed to a glass. "Uncle!" he said peremptorily. But Anisetta turned upon Uncle Giorgio.

"Don't you dare give my husband another drop!" she said. "You ought to know better. My Aquila can't ever stand more than one glass and I think it's a shame for a man of your age to get a nice, clean-living young man like Aquila into silly habits."

She banged the cork into the bottle.

"Silly habits for silly husbands," said Aquila, looking once more at his boots. "Silly habits for silly Sicilians." He hung his head almost to his knees.

"Aquila!" said Anisetta in alarm, "you're not going to be drunk, are you?"

Aquila shook his head.

"No."

"Aquila, look at me!"

"No."

"Aquila, do as I say."

"It's all right," said Aquila in a muffled voice. "I'm not going to be drunk. But I think I'm going to cry."

Then he did look up, and at Anisetta, who saw two great tears dangling in his eyes.

"Oh, *Aquila,* my poor dear!" she said. She jumped up and

standing behind him, put her arms round his neck and laid her cheek on his curling black hair.

"Oh Uncle, how could you do such a thing," she said, shooting a fierce glance at Giorgio through the tangle of Aquila's curls.

"It *was* such a nice wedding," sobbed Aquila.

"It was the most beautiful wedding in the world," said Anisetta.

"And I am *such* a silly husband," said Aquila.

"You are the most wonderful husband who ever lived," said Anisetta, kissing his forehead.

"And I don't want to di-di-di-vorce you," sobbed Aquila.

"Of course you don't want to divorce me," said Anisetta, taking his pocket-handkerchief out of his jacket pocket and drying his eyes. "And what's more I wouldn't let you do it if you did. Why do you think I am living with three men?"

"I dunno," sniffed Aquila. "Why?"

"Because I love you," said Anisetta. "Now do you understand?"

Aquila hesitated.

"Yes," he said firmly.

Thus, in one word, he gave up the pursuit of reason and settled down to be a good husband.

*   *   *

"I do love you," said Aquila a little later.

"And I love you," said Anisetta.

"So you'll come away from here and live with me, then?" said Aquila.

"Yes," said Anisetta.

"When?"

"Oh, as soon as you can arrange it. It won't take long. You only have to draw blood."

"Draw whose blood?" asked Aquila.

"The Marquis' blood," said Anisetta.

"Whatever for?" said Aquila.

"Because he's a nice man really and I think his mother would be upset if you killed him."

"But I've no intention of killing him," said Aquila, in astonishment.

"Well, remember that and don't get carried away in the heat of the thing," said Anisetta, wagging a finger at him.

"What thing?"

"Why the duel, of course."

"*Duel?*" said Aquila, his voice rising above the register suitable to a fully-grown husband. "What duel?"

"The duel that you're going to fight with the Marquis, silly," said Anisetta. "Didn't you read my postcard? Oh, no, I remember now. You didn't. Well," she said turning to Uncle Giorgio, "tell him."

"Are you sure?" he asked. But Anisetta said, "Tell him."

"She said," Uncle Giorgio explained to Aquila, "that she would not go back to you unless you fought a duel for her."

"Rheumatism or no rheumatism," added Anisetta.

"I don't think you said that on the postcard," said Giorgio reproachfully.

"No," Anisetta agreed, "there wasn't room. But I thought it."

"But why do you want me to fight a duel?" asked Aquila.

"Because," said Anisetta with decision, "I am a Female Heathenist and my greatest pleasure in life is to know that I have a brave husband who will fight for my honor."

"But that's so old-fashioned," protested Aquila.

"That," said Anisetta, "is exactly why I like it." She sat down with the utmost self-possession.

Aquila looked at Uncle Giorgio. Giorgio raised his eyebrows, his shoulders and the palm of one hand which means, in Sicilian, 'What to do? We're in for it.' He also pursed his lips and looked at Anisetta, which means, 'And she's a pretty girl.'

Aquila swallowed. He reached over and took Giorgio's wine-glass. He drank it off.

"You have made up your mind, Anisetta?"

"I have made up my mind, Aquila."

"No duel, no wife?"

"No duel, no wife."

"Certain?"

"Certain," said Anisetta. "Besides, I have taken a vow to Sant'Agata."

At that, Aquila knew better than to argue. He squared his shoulders.

"Where is this rat?" he demanded.

"Just coming into the garden," said Anisetta, looking over Aquila's shoulder, "and you do not have to call him bad names. You just have to strike him lightly across the face."

*   *   *

Aquila strode across the courtyard, accosted the Marquis, and gave the astonished man a resounding buffet.

"I said *lightly*," remarked Anisetta, reprovingly.

Uncle Giorgio rose.

"My dear girl," he said, "you must not be unreasonable. I have found human beings are such that it is next to impossible to smack their faces lightly once one gets an opportunity of doing it at all."

"The French manage it," Anisetta pointed out.

Uncle Giorgio replied:

"I often feel the French are overcivilized to a fault. However . . ." He shrugged his shoulders and strolled across to the Marquis who, having reeled against the vine-trunk, was now feeling his jaw. "As my nephew's second," said Uncle Giorgio to him, striking a magnificent pose, "I have the honor to say that we are ready to meet you at any time and at any place at your convenience."

The Marquis stared at him blankly.

"I mean, sir," said Uncle Giorgio, "he wishes to fight you."

The Marquis turned an astonished face to Aquila.

"You wish to fight me? Whatever for?"

Aquila answered him stoutly:

"Because you seduced my innocent wife!"

The Marquis supported himself on the vine-trunk. He took his hand away from his cheek. He opened his eyes so that they were not long, but round.

"Me?" he said. "Seduce *her?*" He pointed a shaking finger at Anisetta. "That . . . that . . . bluestocking! You might as well accuse me of seducing the Academie Française."

Uncle Giorgio maintained his magnificent pose. He said:

"Really? And what, may I ask, is the Academie Française?"

"It consists of forty elderly gentlemen," said the Marquis with as much patience as he could muster. "It is most improbable that they could ever be seduced."

"Then you mean . . . that . . . ?" said Uncle Giorgio, but a little less magnificently.

"That you didn't . . . ?" continued Aquila

"I most certainly mean that I emphatically didn't," said the Marquis vigorously. "I assure you that she will leave my house exactly as she was when she came into it. I wish I could say the same for myself, but I, as you will no doubt have the charity to see for yourself, am a nervous wreck. Who would not be? For seven hours she sat on my chaise-longue, looking as beautiful as a goddess and spouting *ethics*. It was utterly unnerving. It was worse than my mother. My mother is in the evening of her life; a little philosophy is becoming in her. But your wife, your wife, sir, is double-faced. I brought her home in all good faith. It is true that I bandied a few philosophical remarks with her in the Tuileries Gardens. In the same circumstances I have discussed the breeding of horses with an Englishwoman and Benjamin Franklin with an American woman. But a gambit is a gambit. The Englishwoman did not turn my apartment into a stable. And the American woman quickly confessed to a limited interest in Benjamin Franklin. But your wife spent the whole of the first evening—the most important evening—proving, with sophistries that would have made a monk an abbot on the spot, that because I was an Existentialist I was necessarily God.

"Is this true, Anisetta?" asked Aquila.

"Quite true," said Anisetta, admiring her finger-nails. "But I did not prove it with soffilies, I proved it by common-sense. Besides, I don't see why Joel is so annoyed. I couldn't very well have been more complimentary, could I?"

"Compliments!" snorted the Marquis. "It was for me to pay the compliments. It was for you, as a respectably married woman, to call me a ravisher, a villain and a beast. That is what the American woman called me and we both knew where we stood. We had a very satisfactory evening. Too much is made of America being a raw nation. In my opinion their women, at least, have an instinctive feeling for tradition. Thank you, sir," he said to Uncle Giorgio, who offered him a glass of wine. "That is a very kind act. I take it that even in Sicily you do not strike a man while he is drinking?" he asked Aquila, and Aquila murmured:

"No, no. Please go right ahead."

The Marquis sat down, carefully removing his chair away from Anisetta, who regarded him with a sweet and womanly smile.

"You must forgive me if I appear a little taken aback," said Aquila, "but am I to understand that you made no improper advances to my wife?"

"My dear young man," said the Marquis, mopping his lips with a monogrammed silk handkerchief, "after two hours conversation with your wife I had no more thoughts of making an improper advance to her than a schoolboy has when he proffers his teacher an apple. All I wanted was to be let off early and go home to Mother."

"Is that what you meant when you tried to kiss me?" asked Anisetta, with a roguish glance.

"That was early on," said the Marquis.

"And did you let him?" asked Aquila of Anisetta.

"Well, no," she said. "After all, seeing he was Jehovah, it was a little beneath his dignity."

"She held me at arm's length," said the Marquis bitterly, "and insisted on knowing why I ever let the snake get into the Garden of Eden."

"A good question," said Uncle Giorgio with a murmur of approval.

"She had an even better question at 1 a.m.," said the Marquis. "It was about Abraham and Isaac. That finished me. I took her over to a good friend of mine here," he said, and pointed to the apartment with the velvet hangings at the drawing-room windows. "His name is Ellis Peters and he has a turn for philosophy. I left her with him and returned to my bed. In the morning I went over to see him. After all, I was in a way responsible for her. I found her at breakfast."

"Ha!" said Aquila. "Now we have the truth!" He turned to Anisetta. "So you had breakfast with this Peters man?"

"*I* had breakfast," said Anisetta, "but Popsy only had an aspirin."

"He was looking pale and shaken," said the Marquis. "While your wife had not a hair of her head disarranged. Why should she? She had kept poor Ellis up the entire night, pumping him. No sooner had I got into the room than she asked me who was the handsome young man watering the flower-pots in the apartment opposite because she was going to fling herself at his head. I must say that this pleased me. I took it for the first sign of feminine frailty which your formidable wife had shown. But it wasn't frailty."

"It was Female Heathenism," said Anisetta.

"Hedonism," corrected Aquila, mechanically.

"Well anyway, you know what I mean by it," said Anisetta. "I mean . . ."

The Marquis clapped his hands to his ears.

"I know," he wailed. "I know every single principle of it by heart."

"So you threw yourself at the head of the man watering the flower-pots?" said Aquila grimly to his wife.

"Yes," she said meekly.

"And that's the man you ought to fight, not me," said the Marquis rising.

"In due course," said Aquila, even more grimly.

"Ooo!" said Anisetta. "I've never seen you look like that

before, Aquila. Now I know you love me. I knew Sant'Agata wouldn't be wrong."

"Which reminds me," said Uncle Giorgio. "When can I have the honor of waiting upon you, M. le Marquis, on behalf of my nephew? You will no doubt, now that you have recovered from your first surprise at that blow in the face, demand satisfaction from my nephew."

"Satisfaction!" said the Marquis. "Let me tell you that I'm more than satisfied with your relatives as it is. I'm fed up to the back teeth with them. And the only cause I have to quarrel with your nephew is that he ought to show more sense of responsibility than to let a wife like this young lady loose upon innocent Frenchmen. A fig, sir, for your duel," said the Marquis with a most expressive gesture.

"You refuse to fight me?" said Aquila.

"I do," said the Marquis.

"But what about Sant'Agata?" said Anisetta, rising in alarm. "I can't break my vow to her. I can't possibly, Aquila. You know that."

Aquila folded his arms and tilted up his chin towards the Marquis.

"Leave this to me, dear," he said to Anisetta, and to the Marquis:

"M. le Marquis, since it is obvious that you are afraid that I shall kill you, allow me to call you a coward."

"You may call me what you like, young man," said the Marquis, clapping his hat upon his head, "but I am not afraid that you'll kill me. I'm afraid that I shall kill you, in which case, God forbid, I should have your widow on my hands once more."

He moved on his short legs, but with considerable dignity to the exit from the courtyard. Arrived there, he turned and faced them.

"My mother," he said with simplicity, "has brought me up an Existentialist. I have strayed far from the path, but I have learned my error. I learned, if not at my mother's knee, then at least at her dressing table, that an Existentialist must always choose. Gentlemen, I have chosen. I am giving up my flat. I am leaving Paris. I am going abroad for a long holiday—to Africa perhaps, perhaps to the Argentine, perhaps to Tibet. Anywhere," he said with a parting glance at Anisetta, "where women are women."

He turned on his heel and made his way through the corridor, past the concierge's box and disappeared into the street.

*   *   *

"There he goes," said Aquila, striking an attitude, "scuttling to safety like a rabbit." He turned to Anisetta. "Honor and Sant'Agata are satisfied."

Anisetta turned in her chair and looked thoughtfully down the corridor after the Marquis.

"I'm not at all sure," she said. "You didn't actually draw blood."

"No," said Uncle Giorgio, "but I think we can say, as they do in boxing, that it's a technical knock-out."

"I don't think Sant'Agata would know much about boxing," replied Anisetta doubtfully. "But that doesn't matter, because you can always fight one of my other lovers."

"Do you still doubt my courage?" asked Aquila.

"Don't be a silly," said Anisetta. "I never thought you had any."

Aquila went red.

"That is an insult," he said. "And I demand an apology."

"Come, come," said Uncle Giorgio. "You are being less than your usual self. Women cannot apologize. They do not stoop to insults. Everything they say should be regarded as a glimpse of the eternal and unchangeable truth. In any case, you'll never convince them that it isn't. Now, Anisetta," he went on, "I'm sure you didn't mean to hurt your husband's feelings."

"Of course I didn't," said Anisetta. "But if I thought that he was brave I wouldn't have asked him to fight a duel, would I? Because if he was brave he wouldn't mind fighting a duel, would he? And if he didn't mind fighting a duel how would I know that he loved me? I mean to say, it's not much use your husband swearing he'll go through fire and water for you if he's in the Fire Brigade, is it?" She added, as nobody answered her, "It isn't, is it?"

After a little pause, Aquila said to Giorgio, "What was that thing the Marquis called her?"

"Bluestocking," said Giorgio.

"Ah, yes. Bluestocking," said Aquila thoughtfully. And then said:

"I'm glad I didn't have to hurt him. I think he must have suffered a good deal already. Anisetta, my dear," he went on, "if you will promise not to say another word in the way of argument until I have wiped my sword clean on your lover's jacket, I will promise to fight your American."

Anisetta clapped her hands.

"Will you really? I'm so glad. And so is Sant'Agata, I'm sure. I don't have to argue. I just have to shout." Turning to the left hand range of windows that surrounded the courtyard, she raised her voice and called:

"La-ree!"

There was no reply. Once again she called:

"Oh La-ree!"

And Aquila, impatient, added:

"Come out, you skulking rascal, and fight!"

At which Uncle Giorgio said, "Do not let us grow undignified. This thing should be done properly. You must appoint me as your second, Aquila, and I will wait upon the gentleman in question. Of course, he has the choice of weapons."

"That's torn it!" said Anisetta.

"You needn't worry on my account," said Aquila. "I was taught both shooting and fencing at College."

"I know," said Anisetta, "but Larry's college was very progressive and all they taught him was brotherly love. You can't fight with that."

"Oh yes you can, my dear," said Uncle Giorgio. "To the death. But I quite see that it's not the sort of duel that you are looking forward to." He walked towards an iron staircase that led to the first floor. He had a worried look.

"You could sting him with an insult," suggested Aquila.

"It is so difficult to insult Americans in Europe," said Uncle Giorgio. "Since the war they look upon themselves not so much as human beings as public monuments to free enterprise. At least, that's what I found in Palermo. But you're right. It's the only way. But it will be rather like scrawling a rude word on the Statue of Liberty. I shall not insult him personally, I shall insult America. I shall be very sorry to do it, but it cannot be helped."

Squaring his shoulders, and tweaking up his handkerchief in his breast pocket, Uncle Giorgio mounted the iron staircase. He pushed open a French window, and went inside the first-floor apartment.

"I don't think it will work," said Anisetta to her husband, when Giorgio was gone. "Larry doesn't believe in America. He believes in world government. At least he did when I first met him. What is world government, Aquila?"

"One of the noblest ideals of the human race," said Aquila, sententiously.

"Goodness me!" said Anisetta. "If only I'd known that before."

"It could scarcely have made you like him any more than you do already," said Aquila with malice. "But in any case, before what?"

"Before I had a little talk with him. You see, when I told him about Sicily, he said that it wasn't right to make all that fuss about the place where I was born. He said we were all citizens of one world or of none. What did he mean by that, Aquila?"

"He meant—and very properly—that if we all think our country is the finest place on earth, then we're very likely to find ourselves with nothing to admire but a heap of ruins."

"I think I'd still like Monte Tauro, even if it was a heap of ruins," Anisetta replied. "After all it would still have a very nice climate."

"Pina," said Aquila, laying his hand on his wife's arm, "you are a pretty girl and I love you very much and I think it is remarkable how much you have picked up in the way of general knowledge since you left your native village. But I do not feel that you have yet risen to thinking on a global basis."

"Global?" said Anisetta.

"Global," repeated Aquila. "It is the key word of the modern age. For instance, think of all the babies being born at this very minute."

Anisetta sighed. "I'm thinking," she said.

"Do you realize that the majority of those babies are not little pink things with blue eyes but little yellow things with eyes like slits, or little brown things with curly black hair? Do you realize that the vast majority of babies are colored?"

"No, I don't," said Anisetta. "Do the Chinese?"

"What do you mean, 'Do the Chinese?'" asked Aquila irritably.

"I mean does a Chinese mother know her baby is colored?"

"Yes," said Aquila. Then, "No." Then, "I can't see that it's of any importance."

"I bet a Chinese mother thinks yellow is the only color a healthy baby can possibly be. I mean, you can't imagine her going to her husband and saying, 'Darling, I am very sorry, but I am afraid our son will never be really pink.'"

"Of course I can't," said Aquila.

"Well there you are," said Anisetta. "I don't think mothers can ever be global. Of course," she said a little sadly, "not that I'm a mother."

But she could say no more because Uncle Giorgio came through the French windows, and walked slowly down the steps.

"Is he going to fight?" asked Aquila.

"I don't know," said Giorgio, in a preoccupied manner. He looked at Anisetta. "My dear," he went on, "I am rather worried."

"You mean *he's* rather worried," Aquila jeered.

"He is certainly worried," agreed Giorgio. "He has tears

pouring down his face—a handsome face," he added in paren-thesis to Anisetta. "But I don't think he's crying over the duel. In fact, when I challenged him as your second, he merely looked up and nodded, if I may put it that way, through his tears. Then he went on with what he was doing."

"I know what that was," said Anisetta. "He was writing a letter."

"Yes," said Giorgio seriously. "He was writing a long let-ter. He seemed to be deeply moved."

Giorgio paused. He looked from Anisetta to Aquila and back to Anisetta.

"You are sweet children," he said, "and your games have made me feel quite young again. But I have a feeling that this one has gone too far. Is that young man," he said to Anisetta, and sternly, "going to do some harm to himself? I would say that he was writing a suicide note. I am afraid you have been foolish."

"Then I *con*sider it my duty to a very great woman to read the en-tire con-tents of the letter I have written, aloud and in public," said a slow, serious voice above them.

Aquila looked up sharply at the French windows. Standing at the head of the iron staircase he saw Larry, a suitcase in one hand, a letter in the other, and, as Uncle Giorgio had ob-served, tears streaming down his handsome face.

As he stood there, Anisetta noticed how like a big pretty boy he was; Giorgio noticed how tall and well-built he was; Aquila noticed how his hair stuck up, his ears stuck out, his elbows were knobbly, his shanks thin and how above all he could not stand on his feet—though they were large enough—but had to lean.

Indeed, like most young Americans, Larry would never find three foreigners who would agree about him; unless they chanced to be metaphysicians. Three metaphysicians might—in an agreeable mood—describe him as fundamentally a neu-tral substance which was the substratum or sustainer of a num-ber of accidents.

This, though not in the metaphysicians' sense, is not at all a bad description of Larry Loper, who twenty-three years before had been born in Cincinnati.

Leaning from stanchion to stanchion, he came down the iron staircase. He walked, apparently in constant danger of collapse, across the courtyard, and dropping his suitcase, leaned against the trunk of the old vine-tree as though his knees had turned to water.

A single tear ran over the dried tracks of the others upon his cheeks. He gazed at all three Sicilians with such melancholy that Aquila, who was about to insult him, fell silent.

Shooting a bony and almost endless wrist from his button-cuffs, he searched his pockets, found a handkerchief and blew his nose with the thoroughness of a clergyman about to mount the pulpit.

"Are you the husband?" he said to Aquila, but so dolefully that only by looking at Anisetta could Aquila convince himself that his wife was not suddenly and pitiably dead.

"You," said Larry, "are a lucky man," as one might say the same thing to a man who, wrapped from head to foot in bandages and plaster, is nevertheless the sole survivor of a train wreck. "I am given to understand that you wish to fight me," he went on.

"When you are quite recovered," said Aquila. "Yes."

Larry shook his head. "I shall never recover," he said. "My life has been changed. I see now with an awful clearness what a fool, what an utter fool I have been. If I may claim a few moments of your time, I would like to read this letter in its entirety."

"Do," said Giorgio, and sat down.

"Yes, please," said Anisetta and sat down.

"Well," said Aquila, "all right. But . . ." He, however, noticing the expression of intense mental strain on Larry's face, sat down too.

*   *   *

"It is a letter," said Larry in a choking voice, "to my mother."

"'My dearest Mom,'" he went on, reading in a low voice. "'Yes Mom, it's me, Larry and you'll never guess, Mom, what I've got to tell you. Mom, I'm coming home.'"

Larry paused, plainly too moved immediately to continue. After a while, he resumed:

"'You remember, Mom, what you said to me when I left home? I told you that I was going to be a citizen of the world. I told you I was going to put narrow nationalism behind me. I told you I was not going to put America first, but Humanity. And you said—I'll never forget it, Mom,—'*Well, Larry, your father ran away to sea when he was a boy. So I suppose it's in the blood. But wherever you are, Larry, you'll be my son. So wrap up warm now like I always told you and God bless you.*' Well, Mom, I went away and I've been living among Humanity now for three years. I'm not going to say that it was all a mistake. Humanity is a wonderful thing, Mom, but it's not like being among Americans and that's a fact."

Larry looked up from his letter, "No offense intended," he said.

"And none taken," said Uncle Giorgio. "Please continue. It is a beautifully written letter. Of course you must be an author."

Larry blushed. "I've written a pamphlet or two," he admitted. "But it's not my prose style; it's my Mom. You can't help writing well when you think of her."

"No, I'm sure you can't," said Uncle Giorgio. "I wish I had the privilege of knowing her."

"She's wonderful, sir. She's not very tall; she doesn't wear very smart clothes. She never uses make-up. She's got a very sweet smile. And she's got lovely grey hair. But," he said, and tears began to flow in his eyes again, "that doesn't give you any kind of a picture of her."

"On the contrary I am sure I would recognize her anywhere," said Uncle Giorgio. "Do go on with your letter."

"I shall," said Larry, and took another sheet from the packet in his hand.

"'When I left home,'" he continued, "'I wanted to forget

all about you and Cincinnati. I thought that I was doing the right thing. Because you see, Mom, I thought that if everybody was at home anywhere in the world, well, there wouldn't be any more war. You wouldn't drop a bomb on your own home, would you? I wanted every nation to understand every other nation. I wanted them all to get together and talk things out, like we do in America, and give up fighting. So I came to Paris, Mom, and I got together with a few men who thought like I did, and we set up a Committee. We said to everybody, "Look; you say you're Frenchmen and Spaniards and English and Italians, but you're not really. First and foremost, you're human beings."

"Brava!" said Aquila, involuntarily.

Larry looked up for a moment to give him a sad smile. Then he continued with his letter.

" 'Well, Mom. I was right. They were human beings all right. Only I don't think you get the full range of human beings in Cincinnati. Now in Paris it's different. I won't bother you with all the details, Mom. But you know what I am. Once I get an idea into my head there's no arguing with me. You remember how I was at school with Miss Leamington over Divinity. Hammer and tongs we used to go and she wrote 'Stubborn' on my report card. I was like that over Stopping War. I wanted our Committee to go to Palestine wearing white robes and sit down between the Jews and the Arabs till the firing stopped. That put the cat among the pigeons all right and we had a lot of resignations. The Secretary stuck by me, so did the Treasurer. The Secretary is an Englishman named Laithwaite and very well connected. He backed me up fine, in his way. He said he was quite ready to get shot in the cause of peace but he drew the line at being shot in a white robe. The Treasurer was with me all the way. He is a fine chap. He is a Jew. But the President was a Frenchman and he resigned saying he admired my idealism but he was under the impression that Arabs habitually wore white anyway. Of course it was only an excuse. I was feeling pretty low. Then something happened. But I don't know how I'm going to tell you about it, Mom.' "

He stopped. He glanced nervously at Anisetta. Anisetta gave him an encouraging smile. Aquila, observing this, remembered that Larry was her lover, and began to frown. Larry went on with his letter:

" 'Mom, I met a girl friend. She's a married woman. You won't believe that, Mom. You'll say, "Not my boy. Not my Larry." But I cannot tell a lie to you. I knew she was a married woman when I fell in love with her. I knew it was a sin. I was watering my flower-boxes, and she smiled at me. She is Italian. She was in the clutches of a French Marquis. She said she wanted to come to my apartment for a quiet talk in a homey atmosphere. Mom, she is the most wonderful woman I have ever met.' "

"Scoundrel!" said Aquila, and started forward.

Uncle Giorgio seized him.

"Let me go!" said Aquila furiously. "I am going to cram those words down his throat."

"In my capacity as your second I cannot let you do anything of the sort," said Uncle Giorgio with an expression and grip of great firmness. "It is quite against the rules. You cannot fight a man for something you have found out from opening one of his letters. And in a sense that is just what you propose to do."

"Besides," said Anisetta reasonably, "I think you ought to wait until the letter is finished."

"You ought," said Larry.

Aquila snorted.

"Very well," he said. "But you, Uncle Giorgio, had better keep a tight hold on me."

"I shall," said Giorgio, and Larry, taking out another sheet read on:

" 'She came to my apartment and I told her the story of my life. I told her how I had put my home and my country behind me to serve the cause of one world. I asked her to join me in my crusade. I said that sometimes when I looked around me and saw the wickedness of the world and how everybody was selfish, quarrelsome, and lacking all love for their neighbors, I felt very lonely. Do you know what she said, Mom? She put her hand on my forehead . . . !"

(And here Giorgio had a brief but victorious struggle with Aquila.)

" '. . . and she said, "You must have been awfully nicely brought up. I bet you have the sweetest mother back home." Well that did it, Mom. When she came into my room first I had thoughts which weren't nice about her. Don't be shocked, Mom. Your Larry's a man now. But when she said that it was like I was swinging on the gate back home telling the boys I wasn't going swimming because Mom said not to. She made me a good boy, Mom. Her name is Pina but she likes to be called Anisetta which is the name of a flower she says."

"Oh, Anisetta," said Uncle Giorgio, "I'm ashamed of you, lying to a nice boy like that."

"Well, I could see that he was homesick at first glance," said Anisetta, but realizing that this scarcely met Giorgio's point, she blushed.

" 'She came two or three days running to talk to me, Mom,' " read Larry, much moved. " 'Every time I talked about Humanity she talked about you, Mom. She asked for a photograph. I showed her the one of you with the lawn-mower. Then she talked about the garden, and asked me what the house was like. She made me cry, Mom. And all the while she was as pure as an angel and so was I. Besides, I was crying off and on the whole time. Then yesterday she said, *"Larry, don't you worry for a bit about it being One World or None. You go home to your mother."* And that's what I'm going to do, now, Mom, by the next boat. I wish you could meet Pina. But as I mentioned above, she is another man's wife. What a lucky man he must be! No more now, Mom, because he is waiting downstairs and wants to kill me. But don't you worry Mom. I'll be coming up the path any day now. Does that gate still jam? And have a pie ready like you used, won't you, when I came back from High School? Your loving son, Larry.' "

He carefully folded the letter and put it away in its envelope with deliberation. He then looked Aquila squarely in the eye.

"Now," he said, and with considerable dignity, "kill me, if you must."

"I . . ." said Aquila and stopped confused.

"In my capacity as your second," said Uncle Giorgio, gently, "it is my duty to try and reconcile you with your opponent, provided it can be done honorably. I urge you to think of Mom. And the pie. You cannot break a poor mother's heart." he said.

Aquila hung his head.

"Thank you," said Larry, "and now, with your permission, I will be on my way."

He put away his letter and picked up his suitcase. To Anisetta he said:

"Mrs. Morales, may whatever gods there be bless you, if they can bless," a phrase which greatly appealed to Aquila for its rationality, balance, freedom from superstition, and overall modernity. "In any case, I am sure my Mom will."

Larry with a great effort stood for a few moments without the support of anything but his feet.

He walked gravely towards the corridor that led from the courtyard through the house to the street. He gravely turned and as gravely spoke to the three Sicilians.

"Cincinnati," he said, "here I come."

In another moment, he had gone.

*   *   *

There was a long silence between the three Sicilians. It was broken at last by Anisetta, who with a sigh of regret said:

"It's a pity, in a way. It would have been a good duel. I knew he wouldn't really fight, of course, but Aquila could have begun and I could have screamed 'Stop, stop!' and everything would have been lovely. Nobody would have been hurt and it would have been just the right sort of fight for Aquila's rheumatism."

Had she struck her husband in the face, he could not have sprung into action in a more lively fashion.

"Still at it, eh?" he said, swiftly rushing across the courtyard. "I'll show you whether I have got rheumatism or not."

With these words he reached that side of the courtyard which Anisetta had pointed out as Popsy's. There was no iron staircase. Instead there was a neat green door, with glass panels and a white china knob, leading into the ground floor.

Aquila hammered on this door, shouting:

"Come out, you scallawag! Come out you seducer of innocent women! Come out and fight before I drag you out by your nose!"

And there being no answer to this challenge, Aquila picked up a handy flower-pot and flung it through one of the glass panels.

Almost before the tinkle of glass had died away the door opened to show a rather short man with receding hair but a strikingly moulded face framed in neat side-whiskers. He regarded Aquila with eyes that at first glance seemed remarkable for their brilliance and at second for their intelligence.

"Ah!" said Aquila, not moving from his position, which was not more than a foot from the man with the intelligent eyes. "I do not expect this matter will take up much time. I have already had something to do with one American and I understand that you all have an objection to fighting. Well, sir," he said and taking Popsy's nose between his finger and thumb he gave it a tweak.

"I am sorry," said Popsy, "that the hilts are a little battered but you will find the points are needle sharp. I always keep the blades in good condition."

With a proper gesture, Popsy laid two duelling swords on his bent arm and with a sight bow offered them to Aquila for him to take his choice.

While Aquila, stepping back a pace, hesitated, Popsy said:

"You really had no need to break my window. I heard you the first time and I guessed you were Anisetta's husband. I merely stopped a moment to take these swords down from off the wall. It is true that I am an American, but I do not come from Cincinnati: I come from Virginia and so does my family for several generations, during none of which have any of us refused a challenge to fight or permitted an insult. You need have no hesitation in choosing the first sword that comes to your hand. Both swords are exactly equal in length. They belonged to my grandfather. They differ only in the fact that one and one only has killed a man; not, of course, my grandfather."

Then, with one arm still crooked and carrying the swords, he allowed himself a well-bred little gesture of impatience, gently scratching with his forefinger his neatly clipped side-whisker.

"Oh dear me!" said Anisetta in an alarmed whisper to Uncle Giorgio, "I think there's been some mistake."

"Then, Anisetta," said Giorgio also in a whisper and if not alarmed, then very urgently, "you'd better put it right before your husband has the distinction of being run through by a Southern gentleman of the old school," and while saying this he pushed her none too gently towards the two men.

"Popsy," said Anisetta, "don't take on so. My husband didn't really mean to be rude. It's just his Sicilian blood."

"My Sicilian blood, eh?" shouted Aquila, "just see if you can draw a little, *Popsy.*" He put all the contempt he could into the name and simultaneously snatched a sword.

Instantly Popsy, with a lithe movement, got into the middle of the courtyard, kicking a chair out of his way.

"En garde," he shouted and put himself into the proper, if inelegant posture for duelling, the seat well lowered and the knees bent.

Aquila, his face flushed, struck a position which was much more dashing, but which left him open to attack in six vital places. He then caught the point of his sword in one hand, bent it picturesquely and let it go, stamping his foot.

This action, unorthodox everywhere save on the cinema screen where Aquila had seen it, disconcerted Popsy so much that he allowed both his jaw and his sword to drop a little. Aquila's sword, whipping through the air, found no guard to hinder it and flicked a morsel of skin off Popsy's wrist.

Popsy, with an exclamation, threw himself once more into the attitude I have described and in the smallest possible space of time showed that the position, though unbecoming, was nevertheless precisely adapted to attacking Aquila, knocking up his sword and pinking his forearm.

Aquila roared both with sudden pain and fury. Grasping his sword with both hands he flung himself at Popsy, waving his weapon like a claymore.

"Aquila!" shouted Giorgio. "What are you thinking of? Stop the fight immediately, both of you."

"Aquila!" shouted Anisetta, clapping her hands, "Wonderful! I love you, I love you, I love you!" She enjoyed the happiest moment of her life.

"Help! For mercy's sake save me!"

It was Aquila—she was sure it was Aquila.

She suffered the most miserable moment of her life.

But it was not Aquila who cried out. A moment later a tall figure flung himself between the combatants, plunged forward and threw his arms round Uncle Giorgio's neck.

It was Dr. Zichy.

*   *   *

Two things now happened at once. The first was that Dr. Zichy explained between great gasps for breath, how he had got there. The second was that Aquila became a hero.

This second happening, as the acute reader will discern, implies a third; namely, that this story is nearing its end. But this does not happen quite yet.

Dr. Zichy said, clinging to Uncle Giorgio:

"That Communist is after me! For God's sake save me! He won't answer anything I say to him but just levels his gun.

I remembered he was an Italian and when I ran out of my clinic I kept on running till I got to the place you mentioned. Save me! Reason with him! Do something!"

But there was nothing for Uncle Giorgio to do because Aquila had already done it.

When Zichy had flung himself between Aquila and Popsy, he had not been hurt by either of their swords; not by Popsy's, because the American had retired a pace with a smooth movement, and not by Aquila's because Aquila's sword was at the moment pointing up to the sky, which is the habit of swords in untutored hands.

Aquila, startled, had taken his eye off his opponent and taken a swift look around him to see what had happened. He saw the entrance to the corridor; he saw Chichu Bambara emerge from it and he saw Chichu raise his pistol.

The next second his sword was no longer pointing at the sky but straight at Chichu Bambara's throat.

"Drop your gun," said Aquila.

Chichu, brought to a standstill within a centimetre of the point of Aquila's sword, swallowed hard, thus further endangering his Adam's apple. But he did not drop the gun. Instead, his eyes fixed upon Aquila's face, he deliberately curled his finger round the trigger.

"Drop your gun," said Aquila, speaking very clearly, "or I shall run this sword through your throat. I will not have you frightening a lady in my presence, especially when the lady is my wife."

He advanced the point of his sword three quarters of a centimetre nearer Bambara's throat.

Bambara dropped the gun.

Popsy, with a quick movement of his sword, flicked it towards him and picked it up.

Zichy sat down heavily in a chair muttering what might have been a psychometrical formula or what might have been a prayer.

Anisetta ran to her husband seized his head between her

hands and showered kisses on him, each of them being regis-
tered as a sort of pointer reading by the sword that cavorted
dangerously in front of Bambara's neck.

A squeal from Bambara (the result of an unusually violent
pointer reading) brought Anisetta to earth.

"You have jabbed him in the neck," said Anisetta proudly.
"Are you going to kill him?"

"Yes," said Zichy urgently. "You could say you did it in
self-defense."

"Is he mad?" asked Anisetta, curiously surveying her husband's prisoner.

"On the contrary," said Uncle Giorgio. "Thanks to Dr.
Zichy here, he is one of the sanest men alive. He is socially
adjusted to perfection." And he briefly narrated what he knew
about Bambara and what he knew about Zichy.

Zichy listened to this with great impatience. Finally, after
several attemps, he managed to break in on Giorgio's story.

"This is not the time for clinical case-histories," he said, un-
consciously echoing the irritation which Aquila had so often
shown to Uncle Giorgio's placid observations (although he was
never to do so again). Zichy thumped the table.

"Call the police," he demanded. "Have the man locked
up!"

"No," said Anisetta.

"What?" shouted Zichy. "What do you mean, 'No'?"

"I mean 'Don't call the police,'" said Anisetta patiently.

"Why?" said Zichy, with no patience at all.

"Because I am hiding from them," said Anisetta. "For
passing forged money."

Zichy held his curly head in his hands.

"I have escaped from a murderer only to fall into a den of
counterfeiters," he moaned.

"Don't be silly," said Anisetta. "This isn't a den. It's a very
pretty courtyard. And I am not a counterfeiter."

"No," said Popsy.

"I beg your pardon then," said Zichy, with a struggle to
keep his manners.

"It's her *uncle* who is the counterfeiter," said Popsy. "She told me all about it."

"Oh," said Zichy. And then he said, again, but with no more real expression than at first, "Oh."

"Yes," Anisetta went on. "I'm not a counterfeiter because I can't draw for toffee. But I am a Female Heathenist."

"A what?" said Zichy desperately.

"A female hedonist," repeated Giorgio patiently.

"And who are you?"

"Her uncle."

"The counterfeiter, I presume?" said Zichy.

"You are stupid," said Anisetta. "He's not a counterfeiter. You seem to have counterfeiting on the brain."

"I beg *your* pardon then," said Zichy in a confused manner to Giorgio. "I am relieved to find I am among respectable people."

"That's better," said Anisetta. "I must say that a little while ago I thought you were a very rude man. Especially since you owe your life to my husband. But still, I suppose you couldn't be expected to know that in Sicily my uncle is a very famous man. This uncle, I mean," she said, pointing to Giorgio.

"I am most pleased to make your acquaintance," said Zichy. "Mr. . . . er . . ."

"Giorgio Morales," said Giorgio with a little bow.

"Sicily's premier brigand," said Anisetta proudly.

Zichy rose and shook hands. Then he said:

"I am a little confused. It is due to the surprising events of this morning. But—correct me if I am wrong—did you say 'brigand'?"

"I said 'Sicily's premier brigand,'" said Anisetta.

"Oh come now," said Giorgio modestly.

But Zichy said nothing. He merely sat down heavily once again on the chair from which he had but recently risen.

"Well, you *are* when you're working," said Anisetta to Giorgio.

"Then," said Zichy scarcely above a whisper. "You are not a brigand now?"

"No," said Giorgio. "I am having a holiday."

"I understand," said Zichy and never did a man's face so belie his words. "A holiday-making brigand. That of course is very different." He turned to Popsy. His lips trembled.

"And you sir," he said. "You are . . . ?" His tone was that of a man who meeting a horrid spectre on a lonely road, wishes to confirm what he knows to be too terribly true.

"I am the first President of the League for the Uplift of Women," said Popsy. "And I should be proud to add so distinguished a name as Dr. Zichy's to my Committee. You are looking a little puzzled, sir, not to say distressed. That is probably because Anisetta here—Mrs. Morales—described herself as a Female Hedonist. But that is more or less my responsibility: and I may say that as President of the Society for the Uplift of Women I am proud to welcome as the first convert to our principles the niece of a famous Sicilian public character."

"How nicely you talk, Popsy," said Anisetta admiringly: while Zichy said, but to himself, "It is not true. It is all a dream. I shall wake up soon and find myself happily putting it all down in my notebook."

"It is all really quite simple," said Popsy, "if you will kindly allow me to explain."

Zichy did not answer. He merely rocked his head from side to side.

"Excuse me," said Bambara.

"Well?" said Popsy, not too pleased at being interrupted at the very outset of what he had to say.

"If you are going to make a speech, may I sit down?"

"I am not going to make a speech. I am going to make an explanation. But I think you may sit down. In fact," he added, "I think it is probably a good idea if we all did."

They followed his advice. Aquila sat next to Bambara, keeping the point of his sword pointed at Bambara's throat. But the precaution was not necessary. As a well-trained Communist, Bambara had no intention whatever of leaving anything which smacked of a committee meeting. He sat down eagerly.

"Now," said Popsy, laying aside his sword and grasping the lapels of his coat. "You, Dr. Zichy, find events a little confusing, but I assure you they are all quite logical. Let us begin at the beginning. The world is in a dreadful state. A young man," and he bowed towards Aquila, "with a social conscience desires to do his best to put it right. He goes abroad in search of knowledge, a very proper thing to do. But he is not only blessed with a social conscience. He is blessed with a pretty wife." And here he bowed to Anisetta. "His wife, impatient of his slow, masculine thinking, runs away with England's leading philosopher." And to everyone's astonishment he bowed towards the corridor to which all but he had their backs.

"Thank you," said a pleasant voice and, with a happy smile on his face, Professor Lissom, playing with a piece of string, came into the courtyard.

"Lissom!" exclaimed Zichy.

"Frankie!" exclaimed Anisetta.

"My dear Professor," exclaimed Aquila.

"How opportune!" exclaimed Uncle Giorgio, who, like other observant and thoughtful people, marvelled at the way that real life so often took on the shape of artistically written books.

Chichu Bambara said nothing, but producing pencil and paper took copious notes. Then all save he said: "How did *you* get here?"

"After this young gentleman had chased Dr. Zichy all round the sanatorium," said Lissom, sitting down on a vacant chair, "there was some confusion and I found my door unlocked. So I took a short stroll in some back streets. Then, whom should I meet but Dr. Zichy? I had no time to greet him since he was dodging from doorway to doorway. Very soon I saw our young friend. If I believed in cause and effect, which," he said, raising a finger, "I no longer do, I would have said that Dr. Zichy was running away from this young man for dear life. That is the sort of snap judgment which I used to make before I fell into the charming company of Mrs. Morales. But I now know better. I therefore followed the young man more or less to prove my theory that you cannot have theories. How right I was! So far from running away for his life, Dr. Zichy was merely hurrying towards a small drinking party held, most charmingly in the open air. But I interrupted you," he said to Popsy. Then turning to Uncle Giorgio he said, "I seem to have inadvertently bound my wrists together with this piece of string. I wonder if you would disentangle me."

While Uncle Giorgio did this, Popsy resumed: "As I was about to say, in due course Mrs. Morales grew impatient with Professor Lissom who, although a leading thinker, is still affected with that masculine slowness of wit to which I have already referred."

"Hear, hear," said Lissom, massaging his wrists.

"By a series of contacts which I shall not go into, Anisetta finally met me, the one man in the world who really understood her. As President and Founder of the Society for the Uplift of Women, I have long believed that the whole future of the human race, intellectual, moral and certainly spiritual, lies with what is so foolishly called the Weaker Sex. Look around you with objective eyes and you will see that I am right. Observe how steadily, remorselessly, they are capturing literature, painting, drama, the signposts of civilization. In my own country their word is law on a thousand topics. Nay, more than law. Some Americans break the law but what American disobeys his wife? Gentlemen, today America; tomorrow the world. It is the will of God that we yield to women. It must be, otherwise, if I may say it with all reverence, He would not have made so many of them."

"No," he continued, "there is no use fighting the plain will of Providence. I submit to it. I have found peace in doing so. I have found a mission in life. Because no sooner had I discovered the great secret that the human race is destined to be led by women than another discovery burst upon me. I discovered that women are really not much better than animals."

"Oh, I say," protested Aquila, but Popsy swept his interruption aside with:

"I mean no disrespect. I do not intend to be unchivalrous.

I merely state a biological fact. Way back in the steamy ages of evolution a gigantosauros, looking down at a mammal scuttling from under his toe-nail, would have been justified in saying that it was really no better than a rat. But it was destined to become the king of creation. Gentlemen, we are the gigantosauros. Anisetta, you are the animal that is destined to become, not Creation's King, but its Queen. Gentlemen, what did the gigantosauros do? It sat on its rump in the mud and held its head in the air. Let us not follow its example lest we share its fate. Let us stoop humbly to our future mistresses and help them all we can towards their magnificent destiny. The Society for the Uplift of Women has no difficult membership rules. All you have to do is to put your signature in the space provided by this short statement of aims and objects," and here, rising, he passed round some small printed cards, "and there is no subscription because I am not only the President but also the Treasurer and I am as rich as the inside of a dog."

"A what?" whispered Aquila to Giorgio.

"A dog," Giorgio whispered back. "It is an idiom common in the Southern States."

"Really?" whispered Aquila. "A most interesting man, don't you think? Ah! Thank you," he said aloud as Popsy put a card in his hand, and he fell to studying it.

"If you'll all just run through the portion in black type on the front," said Popsy, "you will see that the objects of the Society are set out in plain and straightforward terms."

"I have a pain in my head and a buzzzing in my ears," said Zichy in a low voice to Lissom. "I think I am losing my mind."

"It's only just beginning," said Lissom. "You heard him mention dogs? That's how I started. The thing to do is just to let yourself *go*."

"Each male member," continued Popsy, "simply binds himself to instruct, improve, elevate and refine the mind of any woman with whom, by accident or design, he may find himself in contact. Thus, on meeting Anisetta here, I gave her a brief résumé of ethics, and of a few metaphysical theories. And though I says it as shouldn't, Anisetta is now the first Female Hedonist in the world. Are there any questions?"

Aquila began: "While admiring the general tone of your pamphlet, I don't quite think you have allowed for . . . ."

Chichu Bambara, gently pushing away the point of the sword began:

"Under a bourgeois system no doubt . . ."

Uncle Giorgio began:

"I've always thought . . ."

But since they were all talking together it was difficult to make out what they had to say and in any case Anisetta in a voice which can only be described as a roar, said:

"STOP!"

*   *   *

They all stopped.

Anisetta rose and putting her hands on her hips said:

"I think you are all *potty*. I think that all men are potty. But they're nice. So it doesn't matter. But it's time for someone to introduce a little sense into things. If you think that I've been gazing into your eyes," and she turned to Aquila, "or yours," and she turned to Lissom, "or yours," and she turned to Popsy, "and drinking in every word you said because I believed you knew what you were talking about, then you're even pottier than I took you for. I did it to Aquila because I loved him and I did it to all the rest of you, Frankie, Joel, Larry and Popsy, because I wanted to make Aquila jealous. And, thanks be to Sant'Agata, I did make him jealous and he's fought a duel and drawn blood and now I know he loves me. I've got my own way just as I knew I would. You all looked down on me because I was a simple ignorant woman. But I warned you. I kept telling you to read the Bible. What was Eve doing while Adam was rushing up and down the Garden of Eden naming all the animals? She was sitting under an apple tree with a silly look on her face . . . plotting. And before anybody knew where they were she'd had Cain and Abel and nothing's ever been the same since. And it's the same here. Aquila was so busy telling

everybody what to do and what to think, that he didn't have
time to notice that he was doing exactly what *I* wanted him to
do. But enough's as good as a feast and if I haven't taught
Aquila by now that all the books in the world won't tell him
the tricks that even one single silly human being like me will get
up to—much less the whole human race—*well*," she said
breathlessly, "then all I can say is he'll never learn. So you
needn't go making yourselves giantoporouses or anything of the
sort on *my* behalf, because as soon as somebody lends me
enough money that's not made by Uncle Domenico to buy
my ticket, I am going straight back to Sicily, where I shall live
in peace and quiet and never, never be a Female Heathenist
again."

There was a silence. Then Popsy said in a reverent voice.

"If Nietzsche had met Superman he would, I have no
doubt, have been quite at a loss as to what he should do. I have
the privilege of meeting the first Superwoman. Unlike Nietzsche
I know exactly what to do. I hereby announce that the Society
for the Uplift of Women has opened a fresh-air fund to which
I shall have the great pleasure of contributing the price of a
ticket to Sicily for Anisetta . . . "

"Thank you, Popsy," she said.

"And Aquila?" went on Popsy.

"Thank you, yes," said Aquila. "She's right, you know.
I'm a damned fool and besides I love her."

"And Giorgio?" continued Popsy.

"Thank you, yes. It's time I was back. I'm beginning to
miss the boys," he said a little wistfully.

Professor Lissom looked up from his piece of string.

"Going?" he said. "I'm so sorry. But perhaps you're right.
In any case, if you are going you would be wise to go quickly.
When I left the sanatorium Dr. Zichy's efficient nurse had rung
the police to send out search parties, one of which, if I am not
greatly mistaken, was at the end of this street when I came
in to join you."

"The police!" said Anisetta. "They mustn't catch me!"

"Quick," said Popsy. "Into my apartment. There's a back

door onto an alleyway. Here, take my wallet! All three of you make for Marseilles and call every day at a restaurant on the waterfront called 'La Siciliana.' I shall join you there and get you aboard a ship. Follow me!"

He disappeared through his front door. Anisetta made pell-mell after him and so did Aquila. But suddenly he stopped.

"The Communist!" he said. "What shall we do about him?"

Then for the last time Giorgio saved the occasion.

"Leave him to me," he said and taking Chichu's revolver by the barrel, approached Chichu at a run, his weapon raised.

"No!" said Aquila. "No violence!"

Anisetta turned in the door.

"Aquila!" she said, stamping her foot.

Aquila blushed and hung his head.

"I'm sorry, my dear," he mumbled. He followed Anisetta into the house.

So, after a short interval, did Uncle Giorgio.

*   *   *

Dr. Zichy and Professor Lissom, alone in the courtyard save for Chichu Bambara, looked down on Chichu's prostrate body.

In a voice hoarse with nervous strain, Dr. Zichy asked:

"How long will it be before he comes round?"

"About ten minutes, I should say," said Lissom placidly.

"It is wonderful how calm you are," said Zichy, his hands trembling. "It would be a great help to me if you could go over the extraordinary events of today slowly and methodically, in as convincing and matter-of-fact voice as you can manage. I would find it very soothing." He looked appealingly at Lissom.

Lissom, putting away his string, said, "Very well. But I had better begin at the beginning, that is to say, I had better begin with the dogs."

"Dogs," repeated Zichy with trembling lips. "Yes, please begin with the dogs."

"I shall," said Lissom. "But you had better take me back to your sanatorium and I can tell you the whole story on the way. After all you are the doctor and I am the patient, you know."

Zichy laid a shaking hand on Lissom's arm.

"Do not let us quibble," he said. "Let us toss for it."

And as Chichu Bambara was at that moment stirring a little and giving a sigh, they left the courtyard.

CHAPTER X

THE WISDOM OF THE EAST

Popsy was as good as his word. But it cannot be said that Aquila was the same. When Popsy put them secretly aboard a small ship leaving for Messina, Aquila promised Anisetta that never again would he try to save the world, or be a philosopher, or be progressive.

But on the first night out Aquila, strolling round the small deck, saw two Indian seamen in the foc'sle. One was a Mohammedan and he was kneeling on a mat saying his evening prayers. The other was a Hindu and he was sitting on his haunches, doing the same thing.

Aquila was thunderstruck.

"Fool that I am to seek wisdom in the West!" he said. "I should have gone to India. I should have sat at the feet of sages and gurus and learned the secrets of the Infinite. One has but to look at the tranquility that rests upon the faces of these two men, the resignation, the peaceableness, the utter contentment to know that truth is still to be found where mankind found it first—in the East."

He immediately resolved that the very next morning he would, unknown to Anisetta, make friends with the two men.

*　　*　　*

But unfortunately that night a dispute arose between the two Indian sailors over the merits of eating or not eating cow's flesh as a means to attaining Paradise.

One killed the other in a knife-fight, the killer himself not long after dying of his wounds.

The two seamen were buried at sea during the night, off the coast of Sicily.

Acute listeners, however, heard not two but three splashes, the third being made by Uncle Giorgio as he slipped overboard to swim to the coast.

It was, as Giorgio later remarked to his brigands (who were overjoyed at seeing him back), a chilly method of returning to his native land, but admirably inconspicuous.

CHAPTER XI

THE PLEASURES OF IGNORANCE

A year passed.

Monte Tauro was blessed with twelve months of Uncle Giorgio's government; Aquila and Anisetta were blessed with a son. They had bought a small white house with orange trees in the garden, and when their son was born, Anisetta put a beautifully painted tile in the front wall. It showed Sant'Agata with three breasts; one her own, the other miraculous, and a third held up in a pair of pincers for the instruction of the faithful. On the fourth of February they put flowers underneath Sant'Agata to show that they remembered that it was the eve of her feast day.

Another year passed and again it was the fourth of February. Aquila was in the garden counting the oranges on the tree.

"Seven hundred and eighty-six," he was saying. "Seven hundred and eighty-seven . . ." when Anisetta came running helter-skelter into the garden.

"Aquila!" she shouted, "Aquila! Come quickly!"

"Seven hundred and eighty-eight," said Aquila calmly, because marriage and growing oranges had made him very much less nervous. "Yes, my dear, what is it?"

"Quickly!" shouted Anisetta again, "it's the baby!"

In a moment Aquila had run with great strides through the orange trees and was beside his wife.

"What is it?" he demanded, taking hold of her shoulders. "What has happened?"

Anisetta looked at him with wide eyes.

"Tell me," he ordered, but seeing that she could not find words, he made a move to go into the house.

Anisetta caught hold of him. She found her voice.

"I'm terribly sorry," she said, "but something awful has happened. Baby has got hold of all your books and he's tearing the pages into strips. I tried to stop him but I'm afraid I was too late. He was just tearing up the last one when I found him."

Aquila pushed her aside, and with an expression of greatest alarm, ran upstairs. Anisetta followed him.

When Aquila got to the room in which the baby was playing, he found that it was quite true. His son sat crowing among the ruins of his father's library.

Anisetta clasped her hands together and looked at her husband.

Aquila's expression of alarm slowly faded. He put his hand to his mouth. He roared with laughter.

"What a fool I was to be frightened," he said between guffaws. "Do you know, my dear, when you told me that baby had got at my books, for a moment I quite forgot that he couldn't read them. And now, thanks be, he never will."

With that he put his arms round his wife's waist and picking her up, kissed her.

*   *   *

Thinking of this incident very late that night, Anisetta said to her husband, as she spread her hair over the pillow in a most attractive manner:

"You know, Aquila, I can understand people writing books to tell us how to be like angels, but not writing books to tell us how to behave like human beings. It's a sin that they don't trust in God, of course, but I think it's a much worse sin that they don't trust men and women."

"They don't trust anybody," said Aquila. "Not even themselves."

At that moment there was a loud explosion in Monte Tauro.

"They're letting off rockets for Sant'Agata. It must be midnight," said Aquila, and smiled.

"*I* trust *her*," said Anisetta, "because she gave me an unreasonable husband." She drew him to her.

Aquila knew that when she said 'unreasonable' she meant 'irrational.' But he did not say so; because, now, unlike those days when he had studied the martyrs of Tolpuddle, in critical moments he had no need whatever for pedantry to come to his aid.

* * *

And so they enjoyed together the greatest of the pleasures of ignorance, which is to live happily ever after.

THE END

Taormina, Sicily, October 1948–November 1949